KERRY JAMES
HISTORICAL ROMANCE

TIME ONCE MORE
for
MARILYN
CAPTIVATED & REKINDLED

WARNING

This book contains sexually explicit scenes and adult language. It may be considered offensive to some readers. This book is for sale to adults ONLY.

Please store your files wisely where they cannot be accessed by underage readers.

* * * * * * * * * * * * * * * * * *

WANT FREE COPIES OF MY BOOKS?
Just visit my blog and download free copies of my books:
http://kerry-james.awesomeauthors.org/

About the Publisher

4Fun Publishing, a member of **BLVNP Incorporated**, 340 S. Lemon #6200, Walnut CA 91789, info@blvnp.com / legal@blvnp.com
NOTE: Due to the highly emotional reaction of some people to works of erotic fiction, any email sent to the above address that contains foul language or religious references is automatically deleted by our anti-spam software and will not be seen. All other communications are welcome.

DISCLAIMER

Please don't be stupid and kill yourself. This book is a work of FICTION. Do not try any new sexual practice that you find in this book. It is fiction and not to be confused with reality. Neither the author nor the publisher or its associates assume any responsibility for any loss, injury, death or legal consequences resulting from acting on the contents in this book. Every character in this book is over 18 years of age. The author's opinions are not to be construed as the opinions of the publisher. The material in this book is for entertainment purposes ONLY. Enjoy.

Time Once More For Marilyn

Captivated & Rekindled
Historical Romance

By: Kerry James

© **Kerry James 2015**
ISBN: 978-1-68030-233-2

CHAPTER ONE

Nineteen-fifty-seven was not a particularly notable year for the world, or for the inhabitants of the United Kingdom. Of course, there were quite a few people who would look back and say. "That was a good year, a very good year." But for many it was just another year. There were births, quite a few into poverty and starvation and the law of averages dictated that an equal number died possibly from that same poverty and starvation. In October the Soviets would launch the first orbiting satellite and the word 'Sputnik' became part of every language. This was a shock for every developed nation, particularly the Americans, as no one thought that the Russians had the technology to achieve that feat. We all got a year older, although some, like my mother celebrated her birthday and resolutely remained thirty five, ignoring the fact that she was born in nineteen eleven. The Spartan existence, we had known in these isles during WW2 and immediately after had relaxed and our family along with many others was enjoying a more comfortable life.

Our Prime Minister had told us we were never having it so good. At that time, in our innocence we tended to believe the politicians; later the scales would drop from our eyes. For the moment we went along with this fantasy. Most families had a television now and a refrigerator and if those were the yardstick by which to judge then we were indeed better off. There were jobs for all those who wanted to work and State Benefits for those who declined that activity. The Unions flexed their muscles to introduce socialist principles into Industry. They battled for those whom they called 'the workers' implying by inference that anyone who wasn't unionized was a shirker or a parasite or both. The 'workers' ironically spent more time not working; as their shop stewards frequently called them out on strike for the flimsiest of reasons. The Unions espoused democracy yet rarely let their members vote on strike action. The conflict between the workers and the management was a running battle that went on and on, ensuring years later the almost complete demise of British industry. If we were having it so good, it was a Fool's Paradise. However, for the moment we basked in the sunshine.

It was a surprise, therefore when my dad announced that the family was going away for a week's holiday. The surprise was that I was included. When I was young, we had family holidays. A week or two in the West Country, travelling there by train with accommodation provided by the euphemistically described 'Guest House'. A Guest House was one very small step above a boarding house. The furnishings were better, but the rules were the same, whatever the weather you had to leave during the day and not return before five o'clock. You were provided with bed, breakfast, and an evening meal, no early morning or afternoon tea. For me, the journey by train was the highlight. We travelled by 'The Cornish Riviera Express', the crack train of the Great Western, which, in nineteen forty-eight became the Western Region of British Railways. In those days it was still hauled by a steam engine, either a 'King' or 'Castle', gleaming in Brunswick Green with brass trim and copper burnished all glittering in the light. It was supposed to run non-stop to Truro in Cornwall, but it did stop at Plymouth. Not in the station, but just outside so the engine could be changed. The 'Kings' and 'Castles' were too heavy for the Royal Albert Bridge over the Tamar so they were changed for another, lighter locomotive. It was only later that I understood that during the holiday season there were at least three or four trains that left Paddington in the space of an hour and a half, all called 'The Cornish Riviera Express'. That did mar a little the pride in travelling on that special train. In the mid-fifties, my dad took a new job; moving the whole family from the London area to the Midlands. His position also allowed him a company car for private as well as business use. So the romance of the Cornish Riviera was now history.

For three or four years prior to this, my parents had taken advantage of the burgeoning package holiday offers, and would go off to Spain or Italy with my younger sister. I was left at home with a cash bribe from my father to ensure that I would eat properly for the two weeks they were away. I didn't think they were rejecting me; it was probably because they didn't know what to do with an early teenager at the time. Now it would seem that at eighteen, I was acceptable company once more. Those last three years had transformed me from a gangling strip of a boy at five feet six, into a relatively decent looking man of five foot ten with dark brown hair and a face that could be described as reasonable rather than handsome.

The hotel was quite large with most of the amenities that you would expect. It was situated on a promontory called Daddyhole Plain and overlooked the sweep of the bay and the town. I assumed from the look of the place that it had once been the palatial home of some rich man and had been converted into a hotel with extensions for bedrooms and function rooms. The conversion had been done piecemeal so finding your way about was somewhat difficult as corridors seemingly leading in the right direction would take a sudden turn and take you to a place you didn't want to be. My parents and my sister had rooms on the first floor where the best rooms were. My sister got one of those so they could keep an eye on her she was only eleven at the time. I had a single room on the third floor. I got there by taking the main staircase up to the first floor, walking down the long corridor, then climbing another, less grand staircase to the second where I had to reverse the walk on the first floor to yet another, even smaller staircase that would take me to my floor. The room had a quaint ceiling, sloping within the confines of a gable. From the window I had an interesting view over the roofs and back gardens, but not a glimpse of anything remotely like a beach or sea. There was a wash basin with hot and cold running in the room, but for any other needs I would have to go down the corridor. The concept of en-suite facilities was unknown to the majority of hotels in the UK. That changed eventually with dire consequences for those hotels that didn't adapt. I didn't mind the disparity in accommodation; I got some privacy to indulge whatever my teenage hormones could discover for me. As it happened, I didn't have to go looking; adventure in the shape of the female variety came looking for me.

We had not been booked in more than three hours when I decided to explore the hotel. It was then as I explored that I was approached by two young, good-looking girls. One was I suppose in her early twenties, dark haired, slim, and dressed in the uniform of a hotel maid. She had a mischievous manner about her, flirty and teasing. The other was younger, more my age, still carrying a little puppy fat, but nonetheless very attractive. Her hair was quite long and that shade that was sometimes referred to as dirty blonde. Whilst lacking the wiles of the maid, her smile was very agreeable. The older girl addressed me. "Hello, you have just booked in. How old are you?"

I was startled by the direct question so much that I answered without thought. "I am eighteen."

Did I see disappointment in her eyes? Probably not, but the younger girl looked pleased. It was the older one who told me my fate. "Oh. Well, you are hers." She told me bluntly. I was taken aback by this bold statement yet not given time to consider. Over the next few hours, I came to understand that they had an arrangement concerning any young, single man who came to the hotel. This was unusual for that time when young ladies were a lot shyer than now. I learned later the watershed was twenty. Older than that and it was the maid, twenty two year old Lisa, who would become your friend; younger than twenty and it would be Marilyn who kept you company. So it was that I was left in the care of Marilyn for the duration of my stay. I was quite happy with the arrangement. Initially, there was hesitancy on both our parts as we fumbled through the first steps of getting to know each other, she didn't have the bold attitude of Lisa, neither did I, but once the tremulous first steps had been completed we would chat happily and plan our times together. It was then that she told me that they didn't approach every single young man who came to the hotel; only the good looking ones. Lisa it appeared was the leader and Marilyn followed. I was flattered.

One of the first things she wanted to know was my name. "I heard your dad call you Dal, but surely that's not your real name?"

"It isn't." I replied. "My name is spelt D a l z e i l. It is pronounced Dayeel with a very soft 'Y' and Mum chose it because it couldn't be shortened easily. Surprisingly, she was the first one to shorten it calling me just Dal. That's what everyone calls me now."

Marilyn thought about that. "Well I quite like Dalzeil, it sounds quite romantic, and so if you don't mind I will call you that. I quite like my boyfriend having a romantic name." Boyfriend? We had only just been introduced! If I thought that this was an unusual way to arrange things it didn't occur to me, what I did think was that as her boyfriend, although temporary, I would have rights of exploration and discovering or even uncovering her breasts was the object of that exploration. Yes, I was eighteen and my priorities then were of a very basic nature. Marilyn, it turned out, was also eighteen, the daughter of the owner of the hotel, and had lived in Torquay all her life, consequently she knew the area well. We went to the cinema a couple of times, walked the front hand in hand, drank dubious cups of coffee in various cafés and even went swimming in the sea one exceptional warm day. Viewing her in a bathing costume, particularly when it was wet was very arousing necessitating another dip in the cold water. It wasn't too long before I was allowed a kiss and we both found that to be a very pleasant occupation, therefore we kissed a lot and those kisses became quite heated. I am sure that most young men then would remember the first time they caressed a breast, I certainly did when Marilyn allowed me the liberty. It was a heady experience and my body reacted as you would expect. It was always outside her clothes, though. Well brought up girls in those days were indoctrinated with warnings about being 'fast' or 'loose' and the terrible consequences of letting a boy go too far. I didn't stop to ask if this was normal for her 'friendships' I was too busy enjoying the experience.

As the days went by, our kisses and intimacy became more intense until at last I was able to insinuate my hand inside her bra and feel those wonderful, warm soft globes. I was so overcome with having finally managed to feel a girl's naked breasts that any thought of making the experience good for her, went out of my mind. Marilyn subtly reminded me that this exploration was intended for both of us to enjoy. I quickly learned that her nipples were particularly responsive, and my manipulation of those would bring gasps of delight from her. Marilyn was too timid though, to explore the burgeoning lump in my trousers.

Being the daughter of the owner, Marilyn had access to rooms not normally open except for functions. She wouldn't come to my room no matter how I pleaded. Thus it was that we were able to make use of a small dining room used only occasionally. It was not large enough to accommodate all the patrons except as an overflow for very busy times. In this room we could be together and undisturbed. Here I managed to persuade Marilyn to unbutton her blouse and lift her brassiere and for the first time I could see in the flesh those wonderful protuberances that would keep me enthralled for the rest of my life. I handled them and caressed them, kissed and sucked on them. This was heaven! I was intrigued that Marilyn also enjoyed the experience learning a lesson that would stand me in good stead. Girls liked to be caressed without hurry. I also learned another lesson, that for a man too much sensation over too long a period would lead to a pain in the groin. We were young and learning together, but under no circumstances would I be allowed to take my erection out of my trousers. Nor would I be allowed to move my hand up her leg any further than the top of her stockings. (It was 1957, panty hose had not been invented then.)

Most nights I would return to my room in a state of discomfort in the area of the groin. Years later, I would hear this ache referred to as 'Blue Balls' Very apt I thought. I needed to relieve this discomfort sometimes two or even three times during the night as my memory recalled the wonders of Marilyn's breasts. Even so, I would wake with yet another throbbing erection which would still assail me even after emptying my bladder. I took to using the sink in the room for that purpose, fearful of the embarrassment I would suffer should I be seen walking down the corridor with an obvious bulge at the front of my dressing gown.

It really started as two young people taking advantage one of the other to explore the wonderful world that a man and a woman could create together. Yet whilst this was happening another emotion crept into the situation. I got to like her and she got to like me. Thus it was that our kisses were now given and received with an emotion neither of us really understood. Even so the fact that emotion was present made the kisses sweeter. In the words of the hit song by Jimmy Rodgers that year 'Kisses sweeter than Wine'. I drank of the wine, it was sweet and I loved the heady effect.

Our time together was quickly coming to an end. The day before my departure Marilyn was very upset, as was I. From time to time her eyes would become very moist and small tears would gather in the corners and I too got emotional, but young men don't cry. We were in the little dining room and our cuddling and kissing had become very passionate. I was allowed to move my hand beyond her stocking tops to caress the soft, warm flesh just below heaven. The devil in me urged me to go further, the good angel cautioned. I listened to the good angel not without many misgivings though. The angel reminded me that what I was doing was becoming close to dangerous. This was further than I had ever gone with a girl. As a parting gift, Marilyn gave me a little locket with a photo of herself. It was a cheap plastic locket, but the thought behind it filled me with warm feelings.

Under instructions from my parents, I had packed for the journey home that last evening. I slept with dreams of Marilyn and the inevitable erection. I was awakened in the morning by a knock on the door, anticipating that it could be Marilyn I opened the door wearing just my pyjama trousers. It wasn't Marilyn, it was Lisa. I had seen a lot of Lisa around the hotel; she was very friendly and encouraging of my relationship with Marilyn.

"I have some tea for you." She told me. "May I come in?" My parents had ordered early morning tea for themselves, but not for me, so Lisa was breaking the rules a little.

"Yes of course." I replied somewhat shyly as I was wearing so little. Lisa entered with a tray in one hand and closed the door behind her. She eyed my bulging trousers.

"I think that Marilyn has been a little unfair on you, getting you all worked up and leaving you like this." She indicated my erection. "Lay down and I will help you with that." I did so, wondering what delights I was going to experience. Lisa pulled on the draw cord of my pyjamas and grasped my erection. "Ooh. This is a lovely one. I think I was wrong to let Marilyn have you all to herself." With that, she started to manipulate me, bringing me to a state of imminent eruption. I am ashamed to say that I came quickly, but then I would defy any young man to be any different given the circumstances, after all this was the first time that a girl had handled me so intimately and this was a girl who knew exactly what she was doing. Lisa was quite experienced I discovered and she was equal to the task. At the optimum moment she popped my erection in her mouth and swallowed my spending. I lay there in a delicious stupor; I had heard of this, but never in a week of Sundays could I imagine any girl doing that for me; and she didn't spit it out! She ran the hot tap and wet my flannel in warm water to clean me up.

"There, that should sort your problem." She smiled as she poured the tea and drank it. Obviously the tea was never intended for me! I got up forgetting that my pyjamas were undone. The trousers slid to the floor and I presented myself naked to this pretty girl. She grinned as I, in confusion tried to pull them up. My blush extended further than just my face, I felt warm all over. "No." She said. "Don't bother. You would be astonished at the sights I have seen. Silly fat old men who think that I will drop my panties at seeing them naked. But you, young man is definitely much better on the eye. I should have brought you tea every morning. That would have set me up for the day." I wondered later if I also would have been set up for the day if that happened.

Marilyn waved from a first floor window as I got into the car. I had a lump in my throat and was very quiet for most of our journey home.

CHAPTER TWO

We had promised to write and we did. Every week brought a letter from Marilyn and I replied about every two weeks. Writing letters was not a problem, it was what you said in them that taxed the mental processes and I could never think of anything to say. But as is the way of things gradually the letters eased to once every two weeks from Marilyn, then three weeks then once a month then nothing. I was as much to blame as she, for I had written less often than Marilyn. It was not that I didn't want to keep the correspondence going, but with little chance of seeing Marilyn for some time if at all, there seemed to be no point in the exercise. I am not certain whether it was the paucity of my letters, or if she had found another young man visiting the hotel to keep her company. Whatever the contact, and as fleeting as it was, it fell by the wayside. Next year, Frankie Vaughan also recorded 'Kisses Sweeter than Wine' and every time I heard it, I experienced a moment of melancholy for the days I had spent with Marilyn.

My life went on, the question at that time was should I go to University. My parents were very much in favour of that. I on the other hand, knew that I would be wasting time and money. I doubted that I would get even a minor degree. I was bored with education. Things were happening and there were good jobs available for everyone with or without a degree. Having said that my first job was a mistake from the start. With my mind set on independence I joined a large department store as a management trainee, I soon found out the management part of the contract was quietly forgotten by the top floor and I was simply a department assistant. I left after ten months and took a position as assistant to the Sales Director of a company offering heavy haulage. My father had pulled some strings to get me there, and to be honest, I wish he hadn't bothered, although I never told him that.. The director was one of the most self-absorbed, loud mouthed, egotistical pedagogues you would ever meet. According to him he had never put a foot wrong, and he knew better than any expert no matter what the topic. He boasted of his fine war record, yet one of our representatives who had been a Commando during the war and didn't boast about it, treated the Director's bragging with cynicism. You may ask how he got to this position. He was there because he knew somebody. It was the typical system of British industry at the time; know the right people and you got the top job. Whether you were competent was not a concern. Faced with incompetent bosses the unions found that they could take everyone for a ride, no wonder the UK industrial base collapsed. Of course the irony that I was there because someone pulled strings passed me by; anyway, I was in no position to either create success or failure.

Dissatisfied, I looked around and eventually found the right slot for me. I went to work as a Sales Representative for a well established household textile producer. My new company insisted that their representatives had a thorough knowledge of weaving and fabric printing technology; to that end they would send the new boy on a course of seeing all the work that went into making a yard of cloth. This induction lasted for six months, interspersed with training on the ground. I found these visits fascinating and learned a lot. My interest was such that I then, of my own volition, enrolled for an evening college course in weaving technology. I had found my niche in life. I was busy, working and attending the college, learning all the time. However, I did find time to get married, although I had little choice in the matter. It was a shotgun marriage as the girl in question was pregnant at the time.

Jane, my wife was a very attractive girl who at first demonstrated an active libido, hence the pregnancy. As we settled down to life as partners and parents her attitude changed and she came under the thumb of her mother. It didn't matter that I had a good job, that with hard work I would advance. It was never good enough for her, or should I say her mother. Life could be difficult enough without the interventions of the dreaded mother in law. Our love life became spasmodic and when I was allowed physical pleasure, it was of the religious variety only.

My Dad had an offer of a very prestigious job which would involve mum and him moving up North. I had mixed feelings about their going, but as dad said Lancashire was not too far away and they would be back often to see all their relatives. Jane, my daughter Sarah and I would visit from time to time, but there was no rapport between Jane and my parents, although they loved to see their granddaughter.

I worked hard for my employer for six years and having unsuccessfully applied for promotion I took stock and considered my future. Opportunities for advancement were few, and having failed once the likelihood of another chance was minimal. Luckily I was approached by a wholesaler in the same trade offering me a position so with a minimum of thought I transferred my allegiance. Funny enough, my new employer was prepared to pay more than I would have, had I been successful in the promotion! Life went on its usual bumpy way. My new job was going well and I was rewarded with more responsibility and an increase in salary. In my personal life things weren't so good. My wife and I were not getting along. We didn't talk to each other and our love life, to all intents and purposes was zero. The only serious talk we did have was to agree that our marriage was a mistake and we decided to split. It should have been a simple matter. But for some reason, her mother wanted to make me the scapegoat, by trying to prove that I had been unfaithful. I found out that she had taken to phoning my customers asking if I had actually made the calls that my report sheet showed. My customer records and copy report sheets were filed at home so easily accessed; I had nothing to hide so did not lock them away. It was my Sales Manager who brought this to my attention as he had had calls asking why this Mrs. Amerton was making these inquiries. My solicitor fired off a threatening letter to my wife's solicitor who promptly advised my mother in law to stop this harassment.

After that the divorce went through quickly. Jane's family were wealthy and the house was hers, so I had no spousal support to pay, just support for my daughter, Sarah. My mother in law, far from blackening my name had actually weakened their position. Although Sarah lived with her mother, my solicitor had fought long and hard to get me visiting rights. My mother in law was furious when he succeeded and I made certain that I used every visiting slot possible, probably more to upset the old witch than anything else. Her attitude had no effect as Sarah was always happy to see me, our relationship became stronger and in later years the Court changed the conditions so that Sarah could spend two weekends a month resident with me.

I found a good apartment to rent and became a single man again. Strangely, I was not too embittered, my wife's attitude; by proxy of her mother's attitude over the years had warned me that this could happen, and forewarned was forearmed. I was free now to get on with my life despite the circumstances of being freed were not ideal. As a single man I determined to find pleasure wherever I could. I did and there were quite a few young ladies who were happy to help in sipping sweetly the pleasures of life. I would not describe myself as a player; my associations were usually quite long averaging four or five months. Of one thing I was certain. My paramours were welcome to stay for a night or a weekend, but the moment they started to use my wardrobe on a more than day to day basis, or their toothbrush took up a more or less permanent residence in my bathroom they were gone.

My world went on in this pleasant, slightly irresponsible manner for three years. I worked hard and I took my pleasures as well, learning as I went. The lessons opened my eyes and in addition were very enjoyable as I learned how to please a woman. My adventure with Marilyn had not really taught me this valuable lesson and my wife once married would not consider doing anything that she decided her mother would deem immoral. So I had a diet of infrequent missionary sex with the lights out before it finished completely. For a while, after my divorce, I had a dalliance with an older lady, she was forty eight while I am thirty two. To the world she was an elegant, refined lady, well spoken, well dressed and well mannered. However, once she was naked in bed, she turned into an animal. She taught me much, usually in the coarsest language, telling me exactly what she wanted in her upper class tones. Her appetites transcended what most people would think normal; I was shocked frequently by her demands, yet seeing her in the throes of orgasm taught me that sometimes anything goes. These delightful interludes with her was certainly interesting and informative. I would like to think that I was the only one enjoying her charms, but I suspected that I was not alone

The company I worked for appointed a chap called Gerry Porter as our new Managing Director about that time. Gerry was a breath of fresh air in an industry that was to a certain extent hidebound. He had a revolutionary idea that customers actually mattered. We sold our products mainly through High Street soft furnishers and interior decorators. When complaints arose about faulty fabric there was a game played with the soft furnisher placing the blame on us, whilst we placed the blame on the soft furnisher. The industry at large played this game with the idea that the customer would eventually get fed up and go away. My new M. D. wanted to change that. This was when my initiative of attending those college classes paid off. He called me in to discuss his plans. When your boss, the big boss calls you in, your immediate thought is that you have done something wrong. I was no different. I started examining my work over the last few weeks. Was my call rate acceptable? Was my order rate good? Then my thoughts went over anything else that could lead to my being on the carpet.

I got a surprise. He wanted to make me our Technical Representative. It would be my job to examine every complaint factually and make suggestions as to how the complaint could be resolved should our fabric be found at fault. I would no longer have a sales territory. In addition, he wanted me to visit all our suppliers and thoroughly assess their quality control methods. We bought fabrics from all over the world. We had suppliers in the States, South Africa, India, and Australia and of course most of the countries in Europe. He was giving me the opportunity to become a world traveller at the company's expense. "You Dal, have more technical knowledge than anyone else in this company. I am pleased that you don't have commercial skills as well, else you would probably be sitting in my chair."

I grinned at him. "I could learn them."

Gerry returned the grin. "I would sack you before you became that competent." He went on. "I want you to be completely honest with the customer. If it's a fault, say so, and immediately put in place measures to correct the fault. If you say we have to replace the fabric and pay for re-making, then we will do so. If you say the complaint is spurious then we will write, enclosing a copy of your report. I believe that by handling things this way we will earn a lot of respect in the trade, and our high street customers will push our products, knowing that we will back them up."

He was right. As the news got around the trade our business share did increase as retailers were interested in doing business with a supplier who stood by their responsibilities. We didn't have that many complaints, but the few that were placed I investigated thoroughly. When the customer received a visit from a representative of the supplying company, armed with a camera, Thread Count Glass (a small optical instrument allowing you to examine and count threads in the weave) notebooks and tape measure, they were happy that someone was taking them seriously. Amusingly, this charade worked both ways as a rejection of the complaint was accepted more easily because it had been investigated thoroughly. I also become quite conversant with making up charges and was able to spot the retailer who tried slipping exorbitant charges past us in order to alleviate his factor of the costs.

Since I would be office based now, I gave notice to my landlord and moved to be close to the Head Office which was on the South Coast. I was grateful for the increase in salary as renting in this location was much more expensive.

I had travelled quite a lot for three years in this new job, I was baked in the heat of Australia, India and South Africa, and found my way around Europe. My travels gave me the opportunity of seducing and being seduced by girls of different shades and traditions, a sort of United Nations orgy, and yes, I did join one of those; in South Africa of all places. I also found that Chinese girls are not built differently; as some would have you believe, had quite healthy appetites and giggled a lot during the encounters. It was amazing that two people who had little of each other's language could nonetheless indicate by gestures and actions the desire to go to bed together. The cries of orgasm sound the same whatever the language. I loved Australia and the States. Their cultures were such a shock after the United Kingdom; they were so open and happy. Then there were their girls, so gorgeous and as willing as I to indulge in bedroom games. I was enjoying my life, yet despite all this as the years went by, travelling and tasting the sweet flavours of the sensual life, I started to yearn for the one woman, that special woman with whom I could connect on all levels and walk with side by side for the rest of my life.

In all this time I made certain that I would be back in the UK in order to see my daughter on my weekends. It was a delight to see Sarah on this regular basis and watch her grow up. She had been five years old when her mother and I divorced, as she changed from a little girl to the cusp of her teen years she developed a character of her own, not just a reflection of her family. She was a younger version of her mother, which was good as Jane was a lovely looking woman, however Sarah exhibited one trait that pleased me immensely; she didn't like her grandmother, calling her 'the old scroat'. She was always interested in my travels and listened spellbound as I told her of the places I had been, and hearing about the people I met. I obviously didn't mention the sexual liaisons I had, although she did ask occasionally some quite pointed questions. As if I was going to discuss my sex life with my eleven year old daughter? No, not at all.

The travelling stopped when the company took onto the Board a new Marketing Director, Martin Clarke. He decided that he would visit our suppliers, ensuring that the quality of product we bought was up to scratch. I realised quite quickly that while he knew about marketing strategies he didn't understand the first thing about textile technology. That understanding came after a brief conversation with him when I mentioned the problem of tight selvedge's. He looked blank. Great, I thought, does he really know what to look for? It was obvious that he wished to enjoy the jollies of the travel, whether or not he was qualified to do so. The M.D. was also dubious, but had been overruled by the Board. Instead, he told me in confidence that my position would undoubtedly become more important as our suppliers came to understand that they could get all sorts of rubbish past the Marketing Director. So he gave me carte blanche to examine any delivery of fabric from wherever and the right to reject any that I deemed not to standard. I now had my own department and a laboratory equipped to scientifically test the fabric weave, checking its tensile strength and the fastness of colour in the dyes. I envisaged battles royal with Clarke. I still went out to investigate complaints though.

It was one day in April that we received a complaint from a retailer in Torquay. I spoke to the proprietor of the business, an Adrian Moore. He told me that the job was for a customer who had a large property and for whom he hoped to do a lot more work. This was a usual tactic to put pressure on me to accept the complaint. He was wasting his time as he should have known by now that we would be scrupulously honest in examining the problem. I got the customer's name, address and telephone number, promising to phone immediately. I did exactly that and arranged with the lady a time for the Tuesday the following week.

I travelled down on the Monday and stayed overnight at a Travel Inn. I had over the years, collected a library of town and city street maps, but I didn't have one for Torquay, so first thing I did was to buy one. I discovered that the address was not actually in Torquay but well out of the town and appeared to be quite isolated, so I assumed that had to be a fairly upmarket property. The street map did not show the actual area, but combined with my normal road atlas I found the lane. A problem started to loom as I followed the lane winding around between high banks. There were not too many properties, but those that were there were isolated and all set well back from the lane. Apart from the entrance to a drive which vanished quite quickly between banks of foliage, none could be seen from the road. The difficulty was that few had name boards. It was getting close to my appointment time and I had a horror of arriving late, so I drove up to one of the properties to ask if they could direct me. The woman who answered the door appeared to be the cleaner, since she was local in the place, she was able to direct me. I had asked for Hatcham's Glebe. She replied in a broad Devon accent. "Oh, it's Missus Wilman you want. It's not far me luvver. Keep going up the lane and you'll find it. Look for the bent Oak; it be there to the right."

I thought the Bent Oak could be a pub, but when I got to the tree it was obvious. It was an oak, but bent over the lane almost forming a tunnel; I assumed it was like this because of the prevailing winds. I turned up the drive to the right, which was about four hundred yards long and parked outside a most impressive cottage conversion, although the result could no longer be described as a cottage. I rang the doorbell. I waited some time and was just considering if I should ring again, when the door was opened by a woman. "Good Morning, I am..."

"Hello Dalzeil." The shock I felt showed on my face and the woman smiled. Then a distant memory of a girl with dirty blonde hair, just a little puppy fat and a rather nice smile washed like a breaking wave into my consciousness. I knew her!

"Good grief. Marilyn!"

CHAPTER THREE

Marilyn stood back to let me in. I walked a little like a zombie who had just been zapped by the alien's Death Ray. She giggled. "Well, I have never had that reaction before. That's a first for me." The smile left her face to be replaced with a flinty expression. "Why didn't you write to me? I sent you letter after letter and you never bothered to reply."

What could I say? We were young. Absence makes the heart grow fonder is the old saying, but when you are young out of sight, out of mind rules your emotion. It is interesting how these aphorisms contradict. I said the only thing I could. "I... I'm sorry."

"I should think so." Then her face softened and the smile returned. "It's nice to see you again, Dal." I was actually pleased to see her again. The baby fat was long gone, and the slim figure she presented now is very attractive. Her hair could no longer be called mousy it had become that expensive, lovely shade that they call honey blonde. The smile was still the same, and just as welcoming as before.

"Despite the shock, and now I have got over my mini heart-attack, it's good to see you again, Marilyn." Something puzzled me though. "Did you know it was me that was coming?"

She nodded. "Yes, well sort of. When you phoned you told me your name. Now there aren't too many men in this country called Dalzeil Gorton, so I half expected that it was you who would turn up. I was watching from upstairs, and when you got out of the car I was certain. I must say it gave me a funny feeling and butterflies in my stomach to see you after all these years."

"Not half as much as me when you said hello Dalzeil. You could have said something on the phone."

She grinned. "I wasn't sure at the time. Anyway, you were so business-like and there was no way you would associate Mrs. Wilman with the Marilyn you knew all those years ago. Because I wasn't certain I said nothing rather than make a fool of myself." I nodded. It would have been a confused conversation over the phone. "Would you like a coffee?" She asked.

I certainly would. "Strong one please Marilyn, a little milk and one sugar. I need an injection of caffeine to get my heart beating again."

I followed her through the lobby to a breakfast room that looked out over the fields towards Dartmoor.

"Grab a seat, the coffee's made, I'll bring it through." I took a seat on one side of the table. It looked as if it was hewn out of one huge log about five hundred years ago, and those years of polishing had given it a patina that could never be reproduced with modern methods. Marilyn came back with a cafetiere of freshly brewed coffee, cups, saucers, milk, sugar and a plate of shortbread biscuits. She poured the coffee and passed the cup over to me, then sat down on the side of the table adjacent to me. She raised her cup and looked at me over the rim. "I can't really believe that we have met again. How many years is it? It must be getting on for twenty."

"Nineteen." I answered. "It was nineteen fifty-seven."

"Fancy, you remembered that, but you didn't remember to write to me. You broke my heart." She was smiling.

"I don't think so, you look too good to have a broken heart." I quipped and then changed the subject. "Does your dad still have the hotel?"

"Oh no. He sold it when he retired years ago. Got a good price for it too, and he bought this place."

"It's rather impressive, quite palatial." I commented.

"I like it. He left it to me when he died. I have been here ever since."

"And what about you?" I asked. "As Mrs. Wilman you obviously have a husband, any children?"

"Yes, I had a husband. Richard. He died in a car crash three years ago."

"Oh, I am sorry."

"No. Don't be. I am well over it now, and to tell the truth, he was never much of a husband. I would have liked children, but in retrospect it was better this way. Richard would have been a terrible father. More interested in my money, than me."

"That I find hard to believe."

Marilyn's face lit up with a smile. "Thank you. What about you?"

I finished my coffee before I replied. Marilyn refilled my cup. "I was married, but her mother thought I would never amount to much, so put lots of pressure on Jane to dump me, which she eventually did. I have a daughter, Sarah, she lives with her mother. She comes to me every other weekend. I have been single ever since, thankfully."

"Oh, that's good. A girl needs her father when she is growing up, but why thankfully?"

"My job involved a great deal of travel. Australia, India, the States and so on. It would have been difficult for a wife, being left alone to cope during the weeks when I was away."

She looked envious. "God! That is fantastic. Lucky you."

"Yes, it was great, but it was hard work."

"What did you do?"

"I visited our fabric suppliers to make sure that their quality control met our standards."

"Are you still doing that?"

"No. One of the directors decided that he should do that job. I run the technical side, rejecting the fabric that is not up to standard."

"So you must know a lot about fabrics?"

"Some. My M.D. thinks I do, but I have to wing it a little at times."

She laughed. "And you have come here to look at my complaint. Are you sure you can decide what the problem is?"

I laughed with her. "Well, I'll give it a try."

We chatted for some time, catching up on what happened in our lives. It was such a good time. We fell quickly into an easy relationship, talking and laughing together. I tried to explain why I had stopped writing to her. Marilyn listened to my fumbling attempts to justify my actions with an amused smile on her face. Eventually I ground to a halt and blushed as she laughed delightedly. "Oh Dal. It happens. The probability was that we would never have met again so one or the other would have eventually stopped writing. It was you, but I was asking myself why I carried on when there was little chance of our ever being together again."

"But we have met again, haven't we?"

She nodded. "Yes. Now what would you call that? Serendipity? Happenstance? Coincidence?"

"All of those things I suppose, including business. I am here in a professional capacity so I suppose I should get on with my job."

Marilyn took me through to the Lounge. It was huge! About twenty five feet long and at least sixteen feet wide with huge windows front and back. On the one wall was an Inglenook fireplace with seats against the side walls either side of the iron cradle that would support the fire. She showed me the problem. The curtains were very full and wide. The fabric was a Jacquard weave in a medieval pattern, and in one of the widths could be seen a horizontal bar about four inches in depth where the dye was slightly darker than the surrounding. My heart sank. This was what we called a Pern Bar, where a loom operator had allowed a shuttle loaded with a pern containing yarn from a slightly different dye batch to be used. It was a manufacturing fault. The costs of taking down the drapes and re-making would be horrendous, yet that is what we faced, unless I could talk Marilyn into accepting compensation. I told her what it was, and said that ideally the faulty width should be replaced, if we still had the right batch. If we don't have it, then the whole lot should be replaced.

At first she was dumbfounded. "You can just look at them and know what is wrong. Mr. Moore had no idea. You obviously know your stuff." She went on to question my prognosis "You suggest they should be replaced?" She queried. "Is there another option?"

"Possibly. Would you accept the curtains as they are, but with compensation."

She thought about that. "More coffee, I think." and led the way back to the breakfast room.

Once we were sat drinking a new brew of coffee, she asked me what amount of compensation we would consider.

"You put me in a difficult position, Marilyn. As we have a connection going back years I really shouldn't negotiate with you. Mr. Moore should. I am likely to give away too much."

She smiled. "That sounds good to me. Give me an idea of what you would usually offer."

"About thirty percent of the trade price."

"That's not much!"

"Well Mr. Moore would be expected to contribute on top of that. He has a duty to check the fabric before cutting and make sure it is fit for the purpose."

She shook her head. "He will be difficult. I think he has financial problems. He asked me to put down a fifty percent deposit before he would take the work." Deposits were normal, but fifty percent was over the top.
"What if I were to offer forty percent?"

Marilyn sipped her coffee and thought. "I could accept that, but there is something else I would ask."

"Yes?"

"I would want your company's technical man to make frequent visits to check that the fabric is not wearing out too quickly."

I grinned. "And what sort of frequency would you be looking for?"

"At least once a month to start. Perhaps it would get more frequent after a while." I got up and went round to her side of the table, bent down and kissed her. Her arm came up and around my neck, holding me there.

"I think that could be in order." I remarked breathlessly.

Marilyn was smiling broadly. "I wondered when you were going to kiss me. You're better at it than when you were eighteen. Perhaps another kiss to seal the deal?" This time her lips opened and her tongue flirted softly with mine. The arm circled my neck again and the other held onto my shoulder. Doing business this way was not in the manual, but it was very pleasant. We broke away. This time Marilyn was breathless. "Definitely better. What else are you good at?"

This was one of the longest calls I had ever made resolving a complaint. We went out to lunch at the local pub, 'The Elder" where Marilyn was quite well known. I was introduced to the Landlord and others as a friend from years ago. They seemed to accept that I would be back as they took the time to make me feel at home. The meal was excellent and the local brew superb. I could not indulge too much as I was driving, but with the knowledge that I would be back, I could look forward happily to sampling that brew again.

I drove away late that afternoon, sad to be leaving, yet happy anticipating that I would be back very soon and also the delights I was certain we would share.

CHAPTER FOUR

My report went to the M.D. who was happy with the outcome. We could lay off part of the compensation to the Mill that had woven the fabric, so the cost to us was not too horrendous. Marilyn even wrote to thank the company for our prompt attention to the problem and for settling it so easily. She indicated that as she would be re-furnishing the rest of the house, she would look first at our products to see if there was a suitable design and colour. After that letter the M.D. called me in to give me some brownie points.

"You must have really laid on the charm, Dal." I wasn't going to tell him anything. That it also gave him ammunition with the board was none of my business. I went down to Torquay to see Marilyn within a month of our meeting and on two other weekends staying at the Travel Inn as before. To say we got on well was an understatement. I suppose it was partly our history together all those years before and discovering that we had so much in common, ideas and values. We were getting closer all the time and without talking about it, getting closer to the moment we would share our bodies. I would not be able to see her for six weeks as I was once again asked to go to Australia. It would appear that the owner of the printing works out there had refused point blank to see the Marketing Director again. Gerry the M.D., would not tell me why, although the guys down under were vociferous in their comments. It doesn't pay to act the high and mighty Pom in Oz, and that was exactly what Martin Clarke did. It was a week after I got back that I took off on the Friday straight from work and drove to Torquay.

I had booked into the Travel Inn again for three nights. I wondered why I did that, but my conscience dictated my action. Afterwards, I reasoned that anything else would seem that I was taking too much for granted. Maybe I wasn't as Marilyn pulled a face when I told her where I was staying. "You keep doing that, Dalzeil. I'm beginning to think you don't like me."

"Marilyn, that is far from the truth. If I stayed here I may not resist temptation too well."

She had an impish expression as she said. "My bedroom door does have a lock." She hung the statement in the air for a moment. "But I seem to have lost the key." She smiled seductively over her shoulder as she led the way to the breakfast room.

We had arranged to go out for a meal so she invited me to have a look around the grounds whilst she got changed. I knew the house was big, but the grounds! Immediately outside the house was an extensive Patio with built up rose beds and a small swimming pool. From then on the ground sloped away for something like four hundred yards to the boundary, which was a river. In the next field I could see some half dozen horses, but in the main the pastures were for sheep and cattle. The nearest building had to have been a mile away and that looked like a Barn. As I stood and took in the view, all I could see was the patchwork of fields so typical of the West Country, scattered haphazardly over small hills and little valleys, absolutely beautiful! Marilyn came out to join me and she was absolutely beautiful as well. She wore the little black dress that suits all women, yet she gave the dress a quality that it would not display on any other woman. Her hair was that lustrous honey. She twirled. The skirt was cut to be full and she spun displaying her shapely slim legs, it brought hot blood to my head and to other parts of my body. "Will I do?" She asked inviting, a compliment.

"Marilyn, you are so lovely." Her smile thanked me.

The restaurant we went to was a few miles away, but worth the visit. The area gets lots of holidaymakers in the summer, but this was one of those places that they never get to visit. You have to know the area well to know about the restaurant, but it's worth knowing. The food was superb! So much so that we both concentrated on eating, conversation was restricted to the moments between courses. At last replete but not over-indulged we made ourselves comfortable in the lounge and with a pot of coffee to top up our cups, we talked. Marilyn asked the killer question. "Did you like Lisa?"

I had to think. Did Marilyn know about the incident with Lisa? I assumed not, I was certain that Lisa wouldn't have said anything. So I answered casually. "She appeared a nice enough girl, but I didn't really get to know her. If you remember I was with you pretty well all of the time."

"Oh! I thought she got to know you quite well."

Deliberately, I looked perplexed. "Well, not so well." I emphasised the 'so'.

Marilyn wore a sinister smile. "Dalzeil. Lisa told me what she did for you." My face got very hot. Busted! Marilyn was giggling. "Oh Dal. If you could just see your face." She laughed. Then she continued. "Lisa told me off for leaving you in a terrible state. She said I was being completely unfair, getting you all worked up and not allowing you to...to, well you know."

"Yes, I know."

"Was it painful?"

"More of an ache than a pain."

"I am sorry." She looked at me shyly. "Was it good with Lisa?"

"Yes. But it would have been even better if you had been the one doing it."

She caught her breath and had to take a sip of coffee to clear her throat. Without looking at me she murmured. "I didn't know that girls did that for their boyfriend's. But I think I would like to have done that for you." Now it was my turn to catch my breath. The smile came back to her face. "She said you looked good without your clothes. I had lots of regrets that I didn't see you like that."

"I could say the same thing."

She nodded. "I think I would have liked to have you seen me naked." She reached out and took my hand. "Wouldn't life have been different if we had?"

"Yes. But I would probably not know how to take advantage."

"Oh God! Yes, isn't it silly that when we were that age, we were so unconfident about sex." She laughed and the laugh became serious. "I didn't allow any other young man to be as intimate as that, you know."

I nodded. "I think I knew that."

"Did you?"

"Yes. It wasn't a logical thought, just an emotional feeling. It was special."

She smiled and nodded. "Yes, it was." The waiter came at that point to inquire if we needed more coffee. I told him yes.

The conversation was very interesting. But the interruption had changed the mood and Marilyn started talking about what we could do tomorrow. Funny enough, it involved going into Torquay and looking around the shops.

I drove slowly back to Hatcham's Glebe. The headlights picked out the bends, as always the car seemed to run better at night, the radio was playing romantic music and Marilyn relaxed quietly, occasionally giving me directions. At her front door she asked if I would like to come in. I did, but had determined that tonight I would not stay. She made tea for me as I had mentioned that I had drunk enough coffee for one evening. She had offered a glass of wine, but I would be driving again shortly so I declined. She did have a glass of Red. We sat comfortably in the lounge and chatted. There was no innuendo in our conversation. We both knew we were going to be lovers, but not tonight. The acceptance of that cleared the air of tremulous speculation. As I left we shared a deep kiss. Our lips pressed together and our tongues slipped and chased each other around the other's mouth. Our lips stuck together as if unwilling to part and I was the same, unwilling to leave, but instinctively knowing that very soon we would join together. "Will you stay tomorrow night?" Marilyn asked.

"Yes, I would like to."

She nodded. "I want you to stay, I want to be naked for you, and you for me. I want to sleep naked in your arms."

"We will." I agreed. "Tomorrow. Shall we go out for Dinner? We could go to the 'Elder' if you want."

"Oh God no. They would know within minutes what we will be doing later. My face would give me away. No. I shall cook something for us."

"Sounds good." I replied.

She grinned. "You haven't tasted my cooking yet."

I laughed. "It can't be any worse than mine. Anyway the dessert will be a dish of unparalleled delight."

"Confident are we?"

"I am looking at the unparalleled delight as we stand here."

Contrived compliments are always a disaster. Even so Marilyn smiled. "You do know how to make a girl feel good, but wait until you see me without any clothes. Then make up your mind."

"I am certain that the actuality will be better than my imagination." She laughed.

"Dalzeil. I am not the eighteen year old girl you knew. Thirty has long gone and I will be looking at the big four oh soon."

"And not looking a day over twenty five. Marilyn, I am standing in front of a real woman, slim, elegant and very attractive. I am getting to know this woman who is quite different to the young girl I knew when I was just eighteen. She was pretty, but unformed as I was. But then I had different criteria. The woman you are now is so much more than the girl, and I am drawn to this woman as a man not as a boy." I think those words pleased Marilyn and she blushed prettily.

She covered her blushes saying. "Well, let's see if you still like me when I have dragged you round the shops tomorrow."

CHAPTER FIVE

Men are supposed to hate shopping. I am ambivalent about the pastime. I went shopping for a purpose, to buy food or clothes usually. I know what I want and go straight to the shops that will have the goods I need. For me the pleasure in shopping was the success of getting exactly what I wanted. Women, it seems, shop for the pleasure of looking; perhaps this gives them a better understanding of the economics, and who has the best value for money. I did enjoy the day at the Torquay shopping centre. Marilyn was good company at any time. There seemed no plan for this outing; she appeared to pick at random the shops she would visit.

I had made the mistake of asking her what she planned to buy and she looked askance at me. "Nothing really, but if something catches my eye, then I may buy." Something did catch her eye. It was a dress. Men, as a rule cannot visualize a dress hanging on a rail with the vision it will be when worn by the woman, yet Marilyn had that happy knack of seeing a dress and knowing how it would look. There was one. It was creamy white, quite short with tight waist and a low cut neck. My initial reaction was that it would be quite daring, but Marilyn thought otherwise. She decided to try it on. I have to confess that she was right. She filled the bodice well, the swell of her breasts just peeking over the fabric with some cleavage to delight and entice. She looked gorgeous in it. She twirled for me. "What do you think?"

"It's fantastic. You look fabulous, and your bum does not look big at all."

"I didn't ask that and you're not supposed to be looking at my bum, well not yet anyway. What about these?" She struck a pose with her hands on her hips emphasizing her bust. I happily looked long and hard, looked away, and then with an exaggerated movement looked again.

"That was the second look, and it was definitely worth it."

"You like it then?" I moved closer and whispered.

"Very much, my mind has some very naughty thoughts."

"You have? So have I. I will wear the dress and you can take it off me."

"If that is the case then I shall buy you the dress." I thought for a moment. "Now what about some lingerie to go with it?"

Her eyes sparkled. "Oh yes, what colour would you like?"

"That needs no thought." I replied. "They have to be white or cream." She nodded.

"Ok. I'll go and make a selection. But you mustn't come with me. I want them to be a surprise."

Marilyn cooked a meal of Chicken breasts in Lemon sauce, with asparagus and broccoli. I didn't compliment her out of manners, I thoroughly enjoyed the fare. "You forget, my dad owned a hotel and I had to pull my weight. I helped the Chef and learned a little from him."

"If you can cook like that, I shall have to marry you."

"Yes please." Marilyn answered. And then started laughing at the expression on my face. I was flustered as I had said that flippantly. Her laugh alerted me to the fact that she had answered as flippantly as I had made the comment. So I laughed as well. Later I understood that it had introduced a topic that was probably on both our minds, a topic that needed some serious consideration.

We took the bottle of Chardonnay and the coffee into the lounge, where the fire cradle was heaped with logs that crackled and spat as they burned. We settled in the huge settee and Marilyn leaned into me, taking my arm and looping around her shoulders. She guided my hand to her breast and looked up. "That's better. I have missed your hand on my breast."

"It's re-acquainting with a lovely memory, yet somehow better now than the memory."

She nodded. "Yes, it is. Because this time we don't have to stop. This time you won't be going to bed with an ache. This time you will be inside me, lying on top of me and the thought of that is making me very wet." Our lips came together, opened and allowed our tongues to duel. My hand tightened on her breast and I felt her nipple harden. Without taking her lips away, Marilyn caught my hand and guided it inside the neckline of her dress and back to where she wanted it. Her bra was no obstacle and almost immediately my hand had possessed her breast and my thumb was rubbing languorously over her nipple. Her lips left mine as she gasped. She twisted in my arms.

"Dal, I'm sorry I can't wait. Please, let's go to bed?" I nodded and I held her hand to help her up. She turned to lead the way, as she did I held her shoulders, pulled her back into me and cupped both her breasts. She turned her head and her lips begged for a kiss. A kiss and then another, she became impatient, so with my hand in hers pulled me towards the door. My free hand went to the zip on her dress. Slowly, as we walked, I brought it down. We were in the lobby when the zip completed its journey, revealing the lace trimmed lingerie she had bought. With her free hand, she slipped the dress off; first one shoulder, then the other letting it fall. It was held in place by the tight waist. She asked me a question with her eyes, and I wordlessly answered by easing the dress over her hips. The quiet smile told me that was what she wanted of me. The dress fell to the floor, leaving her clad just in her pretty lingerie, hold-up stockings and high heels. She stepped out of the dress and led the way up the stairs. As she reached the landing, she undid the clasp of her bra, turned and smiled as it dropped to the carpet. She reached out and opened a door, and stepped through leading me by the hand into her bedroom. It was a very feminine bedroom, in Ivory and lemon tones. The lighting was subdued, provided by large candles in tall cut glass vases. The comforter on the bed was already turned back revealing the lace trimmed pillows. Marilyn walked to the bed and turned. She was beautiful; her breasts quivered gently, the nipples already hard that I wanted to kiss it. She smiled serenely and sat back onto the bed, the comforter dipping slightly.

"Marilyn, you are so beautiful."

She smiled with pleasure. "Come and join me. Make love with me please, Dal."

I woke the next morning knowing without doubt that another phase of my life had begun. The warm body that clasped me tenderly was proof of that. The candles had guttered out at sometime in the night, unnoticed by either of us. We were immersed in the paradise that a man and a woman physically joined could create. "Are you awake?" A soft voice asked tentatively.

"I'm awake, but I think I am in heaven."

"Think? I know I'm in heaven." Marilyn replied. "I am lying here naked with my lover, I'm warm, still a little sleepy, happy, and my little lady is pleasantly sore, even though you kissed her better, which was mind-blowing. She has never been used as much in one night before. Nor have I had as many orgasms before. If this isn't heaven, whatever heaven is, it cannot be any better. Are you always that demanding?"

"No, but I have never made love to you before." She squirmed getting a closer body contact if that were possible. Her leg crossed mine, bringing her warm, moist vulva into contact with my thigh. My reaction was automatic and she felt the movement. Her hand wandered south and captured that eager part of me.

She lifted the duvet and looked. "He is very handsome, your little bloke."

I objected to that description. "Little? Be careful what you say, you could give me a complex."

Marilyn giggled. "You shouldn't. He fits me perfectly. What is it men say about breasts? More than a handful is a waste. The same thought should refer to a penis. If it fills me, it's big enough." Her handling had the normal result. "Dal! Do you want me again?"

"I shall always want you." She moved her left leg over to straddle me spreading her legs and settling on my thighs.

"I have always wanted to do it this way, can I? Do you mind?"

"I'm quite happy about it for this reason." My hands came up and took possession of her breasts.

She smiled, lifted and holding me at the right angle, let herself down on my tumescence. Her arms moved up and she lifted her hair from her shoulders, angling her head back as she did. Slipping slowly down on me she gasped. "Bloody Hell. You get deeper in me this way. I feel as if it's coming up into my chest."

"And a very nice chest it is too."

She giggled. "Not as firm as they were when I was eighteen."
"But even more beautiful."

"I am going to keep you around; all these compliments are good for me."

"Funny you should say that." There was no answer for a while. Marilyn seemed to be intrigued with the sensations this new position revealed. Her hips rotated as she sought to excite her vagina in myriad ways.

"Why?" She gasped eventually as she rose and fell.

I did not reply as all of my willpower was directed to preventing a climax. Marilyn's wriggling made it difficult for me to concentrate. With the sensations under a semblance of control I said. "I find it difficult to have a serious conversation when you are bouncing up and down on my cock."

Marilyn was breathing raggedly as the pleasure she was experiencing built. It took a minute or so before she could reply. "I love bouncing up and down on your cock. If you don't like it you should stop letting me see it when it is all lovely and hard. Anyway, your cock is doing wonderful things inside me."

I couldn't say anything as once again I struggled to control myself, determined that she would have her orgasm first. At last I managed to blurt out. "That may be difficult, unless you stop being you." The banter stopped there as Marilyn was starting to make strangulated noises. This I had discovered was how she vocalized her orgasm. She shook and trembled, screamed and eventually collapsed over me, gasping for breath. I followed her very shortly, pushing up with my hips as if forcing my sperm deep into her womb.

When she had regulated her breathing, she raised her head. "Is that five or six? It doesn't matter in any case as that is more than I ever had during my marriage. You lovely man, you do it for me. How do you do that?"

I was still panting and without thought answered. "It's probably because I love you."

Marilyn watched my face for a moment, and then a very happy smile came to her lips. "I was hoping you would fall in love with me, oh that makes me so happy. The moment you came through the front door, I knew that this was important, our meeting again. It is important, isn't it Dalzeil?"

"Yes, it is important, perhaps the fates wanted this all along and now I feel that I wanted this all along as well. I know it's an odd place to propose, but I will. I have fallen so much in love with you, Marilyn. Will you marry me?"

"It's the perfect place to propose. You're still inside me, I'm all wet and I feel fulfilled. Yes, darling Dal. I will marry you."

There are many who would say that proposing in the euphoria of the aftermath of making love is a silly thing to do, perhaps it is. All I could say is that the good feelings I had with Marilyn in the visits before we made love were a sure enough guide. Making love only confirmed those feelings.

CHAPTER SIX

Marilyn had offered to cook me a breakfast which I declined. My travelling had opened my mind and now I would usually breakfast on rolls with butter and a preserve and coffee or tea. The traditional English breakfast of bacon and eggs, no longer appealed. She agreed. "Yuck! All that grease. I used to get sick in the hotel with the smell of bacon and eggs at breakfast time." We sat down to fruit juice, granary rolls with butter and apricot jam. We ate with one hand only, my other hand was holding Marilyn's and she would not let go. "When are you going to bring Sarah down? I ought to meet her before we get married." She stopped abruptly a fearful expression clouded her face. "We are going to get married, aren't we? That wasn't just a joke."

To reassure her I knelt in front of her. "My lovable and adorable, Marilyn. I love you deeply and want you to be my wife. Please say yes." Tears came to her eyes and she brought her face down to mine and kissed me tenderly.

"Yes, darling Dalzeil. I love you so much and nothing would make me as happy as being your wife. Yes. I will marry you." We finished our breakfast and Marilyn with mischief in her eyes took me back to bed to celebrate our engagement.

As it happened, I was scheduled to have Sarah with me next weekend. Marilyn was eager to meet her. "Bring her down, please Dal. I have plenty of room." I was a little dubious, and would have preferred to book the Travel Inn. I wondered about the propriety of sleeping with Marilyn when my daughter was in the house.

Marilyn shook with laughter, teasing me. "How old is she, Dal?" She was being facetious.

I sighed. "As if you didn't know, she's eleven going on twelve."

"Twelve year old girls these days are well aware of what adults do when they are engaged to be married. I doubt that Sarah will give it any thought at all."

She was right; Sarah gave it no thought at all. She said something that I didn't think about at first. "Roger moved in with Mummy very soon after you left, Daddy."

She and Marilyn got on like a house on fire. Their friendship was sealed when Marilyn took Sarah to the livery stables just down the lane. Sarah came back demanding from me that I equip her with everything she needed for horse riding, announcing that she wanted to come down with me every time I came to see Marilyn and she would be riding frequently. Marilyn explained how this was possible. "Bill Thaxton takes in the horses at livery. They need to exercise frequently and he does it when the owners can't. He is pushed to do that, so I go down from time to time and exercise a horse or two. Sarah took to riding like a duck to water, so Bill told her that she could ride out with him anytime she was down. He will be with her all the time so she won't come to any harm." I shrugged my shoulders, accepting the situation, happily when Marilyn whispered that that would give us plenty of time to get intimate with each other. "You can undress me and I will undress you and then you can do those deliciously dirty things to me that you do so well and I can bounce up and down again on top of you with your lovely cock in me." Who's going to argue with that?

Marilyn had picked up on the comment that Sarah made about my ex and her man. In the way of women she had obliquely asked Sarah about that. One night she mentioned it to me. "Dal. You did understand what Sarah said about your wife's new man, didn't you?"

I must have looked confused as I couldn't recall what she was talking about. "Remind me, I can't think of it at the moment." Well, we were in bed together and her hand was asking questions of my penis which was starting to answer positively.

"About Roger moving in very shortly after you left."

I had known that Jane had a man-friend for some time. It would be curious if she had remained celibate. "Oh yes. What about it?"

"It was three weeks after you left."

She had my attention now. "Bloody hell! That was quick." Then I thought about it more. "Too quick. Much too quick." My mental processes were in top gear as I pondered the ramifications. A light went on and the bell went 'ting'. "She must have known him before we split; the crafty bitch was cheating on me! And her mother must have known about it. No wonder they tried to stiff me." I began to laugh; it was so long ago now that anything other than laughing would be futile. "I am so pleased that my solicitor went overboard to get me visiting rights with Sarah. That really upset them." I turned to Marilyn. "And if all that had never happened, I would not be with you now. So however devious they were, I came out on top."

She hugged me and her leg came over mine. "Only until I get on top. I have got all squishy down there, and you have gone all lovely and hard again. I have the perfect place for him." She did.

Our wedding was arranged very easily. I had thought that as I was divorced it could not be a Church Wedding. Not so. Marilyn had no doubts that we would be married in the local church. It would seem that she made frequent donations to the re-building fund. The Vicar, she was certain would agree to marry us for fear of losing those donations. I had thought from the start that Marilyn was quite well off, but as time went by I understood that she was in a much better position financially than I first believed. I discovered this by chance. For old time's sake and happy memories I had gone to look at the hotel one day when I was in Torquay. The building was still there, but was no longer a hotel. The place had been converted into apartments. I mentioned this to Marilyn. "Yes, I know." She thought for a moment then carried on. "I had that done about five years ago."

I was brought up short. "You?" She nodded. "But you said your dad had sold the hotel."

"He did. The new owners couldn't make a go of it; well few can these days. Everybody goes to the Mediterranean now. They went bankrupt, so I bought the place back from the insolvency practitioners for about twenty percent of what dad received."

I was smiling. "Wheeler Dealer eh?"

She shook her head. "No. It was stupid. I bought it back out of nostalgia; it was my home, where I grew up. Once I had it, I realised that I may have saddled myself with a White Elephant. It was then that the idea of converting the place into apartments came to me. People retire and when they do like to live in luxury in places like Torquay, Bournemouth and Eastbourne. They rent on an annual lease. They get a luxurious apartment with no worries about plumbing, electrics, the roof and the gardens. I get a regular income and of course all the time the value of the land is increasing."

Somehow I knew this wasn't the end of it. So I encouraged her. "Go on."

She smiled shyly. "It went so well. I had rented all the apartments except for one within six months, so I bought another old hotel and did the same. Hotels like that were going cheap those days. The costs of converting them to give the customers the facilities they experience in Spain and Majorca are prohibitive. If you put an ensuite bathroom into two bedrooms you lose a third bedroom for every two you convert. All some saw was the loss of a bedroom, not the increased tariff you could charge for having an ensuite. So they sold, cheaply. The thing about apartments is that you get income all year round, not just in the high season.

I was impressed by her business sense. "You said you had occupants for all the apartments except one. Did you eventually rent that as well?"

"No. I kept it. It's mine, well ours now. I loved the hotel, it had many happy memories, and you my darling were one of those happy memories. I go there from time to time to remember when life was so uncomplicated. Now we can go there."

"I think I would like that."

She agreed. "Yes we can have 'us' time there." She had a wicked glint in her eye, giving me a good idea about her interpretation of 'us' time. "My apartment is on the top floor and not overlooked, although it has a wonderful view from the balcony. I was thinking that we wouldn't need to get dressed when we are there, it could be quite interesting."

"Hmm." I leered at her. "Alfresco loving. Extremely interesting." Marilyn smiled and nodded eagerly.

The mention of the hotel sparked a conversation about that week. I tried to tell her how it had affected me, that I left feeling as if I had been shown the open door to paradise, had looked through, but had not been allowed to enter. "When I left I suppose I knew we would never see each other again. Probably why I didn't write too much, I was prolonging a relationship that could never come to anything. So my sub-conscious told me not to chase the rainbow."

"Thanks." Marilyn replied dryly. Then she laughed. "Lisa told me to forget you; she said I had an adventure for a week and to look forward to the next adventure. She got quite angry with me as I didn't join in the game with her again."

"You didn't?"

"No. I didn't understand at the time what was happening. All I knew was that you had affected me more than I intended. There were other young men who stayed at the hotel. I talked to them, but none of them interested me at all. I think Lisa took care of them all."

"I can imagine."

"Oh don't make her sound like a slut. She enjoyed life and men. I didn't really understand what she got out of it." She paused for a moment and gave me a loving smile. "I do now!"

The wedding did take place in the Church. My marriage to Jane had been in a Register Office. Her mother, again, who decided that as Jane was pregnant, it would be wrong to marry in Church and in white. Learning that, Marilyn's vicar was easily persuaded to marry us. This was my first and last marriage in a Church. It was a quiet affair. Sarah was asked by Marilyn to be her Bridesmaid and I asked Robert, one of my colleagues at work to be my Best Man. My Bride looked a picture in Ivory and lace as did Sarah, who like all girls rose to the occasion with aplomb. Seeing the beautiful vision of Marilyn approaching me at the Altar Rail, had my heart thumping within my chest. I stuttered a little when I made my responses. Marilyn had no problems though. I had not expected Gerry, my M.D., to attend, but he did. He used his seniority to subvert the best man and made a speech instead of him. I had to say I blushed at his effusive comments. He chatted with Marilyn at the reception for some time. Later he collared me. "Dal, when you said you were getting married, you didn't tell me that this was the lady whose complaint you went to see."

"Oh! Didn't I? I am sorry I didn't think to mention."

"Crafty Bugger! You can't get results by marrying all the complainants." He grinned. "She's a smashing lady, and wealthy. You have done well. I suppose we are going to lose you now?"

"Lose me? Why?"

"You won't need to work, will you?"

"I wasn't thinking of stopping work."

"Oh? I got the feeling that your new wife had other ideas."

The subject didn't come up until we got back from our Honeymoon in Tenerife. Marilyn mentioned casually one day that the agents she used to administer her properties were costing her a fortune. She then went on to wonder if there could be another way to get that work done. Gerry's words came back to me and I saw where this was leading.

"I am not at all conversant with letting agency work, but from what I have heard it is a minefield, what with tenancy agreements and local planning law. It's almost as bad as being a solicitor. Perhaps you should look around for another agency, see if anyone would do it for a lower percentage."

That gave her something to think about. "Oh! I was thinking that you might like to have a look at it."

"Me? I wouldn't know the first thing about it, or where to start. No my darling, I would be terrified that I could cost you a lot of money and I would hate to have you upset with me. My expertise is in fabrics. The Cobbler should stick to his Last." I said firmly. The subject was never mentioned again.

CHAPTER SEVEN

Jane, my ex wife had by coincidence re-married at almost the same time to Roger. Why after all the years she had been living with him she should decide to marry I couldn't fathom. However, it was none of my business. It was some months later that I noticed Sarah had started to make acerbic comments about her step-father. Later, her language was almost vitriolic. Marilyn noticed this as well and tried to draw Sarah out. One Sunday evening Marilyn broached the subject. I had just got back after driving Sarah up to Bristol where we would meet Jane who had driven down to pick her up. Jane and I would not talk; it was little more than Sarah getting out of my car and getting in Jane's.

"We may have a problem Dal." She called me Dal all the time now. "Sarah has told me that her step-father is behaving inappropriately towards her."

"How inappropriately?" I wanted to know, fearing the worst.

"He touches her too much, and comes into the bathroom 'accidentally' when she is having a bath."

"And it is not accidental?"

"Sarah thinks not. She locks the door, but the lock is not that secure. She has suggested that he has done something to the lock." My anger was almost uncontrollable. I was supposed to be driving back to work the next day, instead I was ready to jump in the car and drive to Jane's house now and sort the bastard out. Marilyn calmed me down.

"Dal! If he is going to go further, he will not do anything whilst Jane is in the house. Call your solicitor first thing in the morning. He can apply for an emergency injunction banning him from the house until we can get a hearing in the Family Court." Despite my anger there was one crumb of comfort in this. Sarah had talked with Marilyn, confirming her trust for her step-mother, and Marilyn had used the word 'we'. This was not just my battle; Marilyn had stepped up to the line alongside of me.

I phoned the solicitor that Monday morning. He had done well for me at the time of the divorce and I trusted him to get things moving. He did. He got a Family Court injunction that day, and it was enforced on Sarah's step-father that evening by the police. As you can imagine all hell let loose. Sarah was interviewed by a police woman, trained to spot the clues. Sarah was a little reticent as anyone would expect; children are fearful of accusing adults; but it would appear said enough for the police woman to decide there were sufficient grounds for an investigation. Jane's new husband had to leave the house immediately. Jane phoned me, calling me all the names under the Sun. Later her mother called me, a call I wish I had recorded as she slandered me in almost every sentence. The gist of her message was that I had been a useless husband in every respect who didn't know how to take care of a wife and I was jealous of Roger who made Jane very happy. She got so carried away that she inadvertently let slip that Roger had been taking care of Jane even before we split, something I had worked out after Sarah's comments. According to her I was so envious of them I was trying to break up a happy home so that I could get custody of Sarah. That it wouldn't work and that she was going to instruct her solicitor to sue me for defamation of character. I tried to point out that only Sarah's step-father could do that, and that the police believed there was sufficient evidence to investigate. I was talking to a brick wall. My ex-mother in law had tunnel vision and an ability to ignore facts that didn't fit her theory.

The Family Court is very different to those you see on TV. The Judge and Counsel do not wear robes or wigs and the atmosphere is without the ceremony and traditional manner of speech. Even so the experience was uncomfortable for me as Jane, her husband and her mother cast looks of venom towards me as the evidence was heard. Marilyn smiled sweetly at them exacerbating their hate. As is usual with minors, Sarah gave testimony in private to the Judge. Eventually it was decided that whilst there was no evidence of actual assault, the Court believed that his actions did constitute a threat. That put Sarah on the 'at risk' register.

The representative from Social Services immediately spoke of her intention to apply for a Care Order if Jane continued to live with her husband with Sarah resident as well. My solicitor took that opportunity to apply to the Court on my behalf for Sarah's custody. Social Services talked to Marilyn and I about our circumstances, and they told the Court that we were suitable. Again the Judge spoke to my daughter in private. He granted an interim order for residency to be reviewed in six months. Sarah left the Court with us. A policeman accompanied us to Jane's house so that we could collect my daughter's things without harassment. At one point he had to warn my ex mother in law to keep a civil tongue in her head. Sarah sat in the back of the car chattering happily with Marilyn all the way back to Torquay.

I could not have been happier in my life. I had a loving wife; a very loving wife judging by the number of times she would entice me to bed with no intention of allowing me to sleep. Sometimes she was so impatient that we didn't actually get to the bedroom. She also had a penchant for alfresco loving. It was a saving factor that her terrace was not overlooked. My daughter was now in my custody and equally as happy as I. When she wasn't in school she was down helping Bill Thaxton with the horses. She came home with a very contented smile and stinking of horse sweat and liniment. Bill had told Marilyn that her riding ability was coming along well, and suggested that she could enter for a local Gymkhana soon, but would need her own horse. I could see another demand on my wallet approaching. Jane and her husband were still together, and from what I could tell were getting along. He was still arguing the accusations, but had told Jane that if that lying, deceitful child ever came back into the house, he would leave. She didn't contest the Court Order when it came up for review. That suited me.

A seemingly innocuous request from one of our customers turned me onto a different path in life. They asked if I would appear as an expert witness in a small claims Court action. They had supplied curtains to a customer who was refusing to pay the bill on the grounds that they were unfit for purpose. Gerry agreed that it was in order, especially as we hadn't supplied the fabric.

The customer had their own expert witness, a guy who taught soft furnishing at the local college. This wasn't the stuff of television dramas. We sat around a table with a Stipendiary Magistrate as judge. He asked the other expert questions and the replies convinced me that this guy knew nothing about fabric technology. When the Magistrate turned to me and asked very similar questions I demolished the other's argument with facts. Our customer won. The Magistrate then asked the other expert witness if he had incurred any expenses and the silly bugger handed over a list. He had lost the case for his client and still wanted to pay for his completely ineffective time. The Magistrate raised his eyebrows, and then turned to me asking if I had incurred expenses. I shook my head and told him no. That day had far reaching consequences.

Four months later a letter arrived. I was curious as I saw the return address, it was from a Solicitor. Now I had learned that correspondence from solicitors was not usually good news. As I read it, I became rather confused. They were asking me if I would appear at a Crown Court as an expert witness. It indicated a conference with the defending Barrister later that month. I talked to Gerry and he said that if I wanted to appear, the company will agree, but there would be a fee. I went to the conference appearing confident, but nonetheless with apprehension. I was surprised when the Barrister turned out to be James Wolstenhome, the magistrate from the small claims Court.

He greeted me warmly. Understanding my confusion, he explained. "Most Magistrates are picked from the community. Barristers however, get asked to act and are paid as a stipendiary. The Lord Chancellor looks upon it as training for possible elevation to the High Court Bench." I nodded as if I really understood this and he took that as permission to go on. "Although I act as a Stipendiary it is only for two to three weeks at a time. I come back to Chambers and pick up on any Briefs my colleagues haven't snaffled. Mr. Gorton, I asked the solicitor to contact you. At that Small Claims hearing you came across to me as someone who does know the subject well and what is more can talk about it in language that everyone could understand. I was astounded when that other so-called expert lost the case for his client and then had the gall to ask for his expenses. You impressed me. My junior has done a lot of research and it would seem that there are few fabric technology experts left in this country. We don't understand why." I thought I knew why, but it was a long subject so I didn't respond to his query.

We talked for quite some time and he gave me the relevant information of the case. I ventured an opinion, but told him I would need to see the fabric and examine it. I also told him what my company would want as a fee for my services. He didn't seem surprised at the amount. He made the arrangements for me to examine the fabric.

The fabric was as perfect as it could be; bearing in mind the comments of the many skilled weavers I had listened to over the years, that there hadn't been a perfect yard of fabric woven ever. That was something I wouldn't mention in Court. I spent five hours going over every inch of it, and I couldn't find anything wrong. My evidence in the Civil Court was exactly that. The counsel for the plaintiff tried to trip me up. I countered by using technical terms in my replies to him that I doubted he understood. As in all trades there are plenty of technical terms and quite a few slang expressions which are used by weavers alone. As a witness, I wasn't allowed to stay in Court after giving my expert opinion, just in case I was recalled. I was very pleased when James Wolstenhome came out of Court with a big grin on his face. He removed his wig and shook my hand. "Your expert opinion did It, Mr. Gorton. The Judge was most impressed." He was about to walk away, but he stopped and turned back to me. "I am sorry that your employer will be the one to get your fees. You could make a good living with your knowledge. Especially as you are able to retain your wits when cross-examined by Counsel. Civil actions like these are going on all the time. If you do not mind I will suggest your name to any other Barrister needing your expertise."

Gerry was very happy with the outcome. The company received over four thousand pounds for four days of my time. Well, in excess of my salary for those days. He took me out to lunch. "Dal, is there any chance of your being an expert witness again?"

"They seem to think so. James Wolstenhome asked if he could recommend me to other Barristers."

He thought about that. "With my company hat on I should say good, the fees will be a useful income, but as your friend, and I hope we can call ourselves friends, you could make a good living as an independent. Have you thought about that?"

"Not really. Wolstenhome suggested it, but it would be something that I need to research first and also talk to Marilyn."

"Dal, the technical side is running well. The lab boys know what they are doing. With the Board backing Clarke, he will continue to go and see the manufacturers, and no doubt we will continue to get rubbish yardage in our deliveries. You will never get any further, I'm afraid. Clarke will block you at every turn. So think about it. If you decide yes, let me know before you put anything in writing. I will see if I can engineer a redundancy for you. That would be one move upon which Clarke will be quite happy to back me I am sure."

"What about complaints?" I reminded him of my primary responsibility.

"No problem. We will have to find an independent expert. You may be able to suggest someone?" He grinned and I smiled too. Gerry had obviously thought this out; perhaps that's why he was M.D. I also suspected that he was playing a long game with the goal of getting Clarke out.

CHAPTER EIGHT

Marilyn was all in favour of my becoming self-employed as an independent expert. I was dubious, concerned that the call for my expertise would not be sufficient to bring me a good income. I will give Marilyn her due; she never actually came out and said that she could support us both. She knew full well that I would not accept being a kept man. What she did say was quite diplomatic.

"Dal, since you have been living here, you have contributed to the running costs and saved me a lot of money. Money I would have to spend, so you could say we are in credit. I am quite sure that you will still be bringing in enough for your share; you are good at what you do. If there were a shortfall, it would only be of short duration and easily recovered when the business takes off. This house is ours, not mine. The blocks of apartments are ours, not mine, therefore the income from them is ours not mine. I am old-fashioned in that way, my husband is my life. You have brought laughter and happiness into our home, especially love. None of that existed before you came back into my life. I want you to keep doing that." She had a mischievous grin on her face as she went on. "I want you to keep doing me, I enjoy that. Do you think we have time to...?" We did and we did. Of course, what man is going to argue with a lovely lady who had a firm hold on his most precious appendage?

I phoned Gerry and told him my decision. "Ok, Dal. Come in as normal on Monday, but say nothing to anyone. I'll bring up the subject of making you redundant at the Board Meeting and we will see what happens." He had a quiet word with Martin Clarke, who was all in favour of making me redundant and it was Martin, not Gerry who made the suggestion at the Board Meeting. I got the notice a week later. They offered me six month's salary and my company car, which was three years old, to go. That relieved my worries considerably. I cleared my desk and said goodbye to my colleagues. Gerry told me in a private moment that it wouldn't be goodbye as they would be retaining me to report on any complaints, offering two hundred pounds for a report plus any mileage over sixty miles.

In the next twelve months, I examined ten serious complaints from my old employers, twenty six complaints referred to me by my erstwhile competitors and three cases referred by Barristers. My income was not far short of the salary I had enjoyed before. In the next year I exceeded that income. I was sure that Marilyn and I had made the right decision.

We were enjoying the rare warm sunny day. Spring can be capricious in the British Isles; always promising to be fair, but so often the westerly winds would bring in cloud and light rain. This day was a gift from the Gulf Stream. There was just a hint of breeze and the sun shone brightly. Sarah was at school and I had just one report to write, so from mid-morning Marilyn and I were able to sit out on the patio relaxing. It was close to half past twelve and we were beginning to think about Lunch when the faint chimes of the doorbell rang. I made as if to get up, but Marilyn beat me to it. "I'll go." Five minutes later she returned. "Dal! We have a visitor."

I tuned in my chair and was amazed to see my ex-wife. Jane was and still is a good looking woman, even if she was dressed in jeans and a sweatshirt she would turn heads. I did think though that she looked a little older than her years. "Jane!"

She looked flustered. "I'm sorry that I just called. Roger and I were in the area. He went to ride on the Paignton Steam Railway. So I thought as it was half-term, I would try to see Sarah."

"Jane! Half-term down here is next week. Sarah won't be back until four."

She heard this and her shoulders slumped. "Oh damn! I really had to summon up a lot of courage to come here, and now it all goes to nothing."

"Why don't you sit down and relax." Marilyn took over. "I was just going to get some lunch, you are welcome to join us, and you can see Sarah when she gets back."

"Would you mind? After all, we aren't the best of friends really, are we?"

I got up, walked over to Jane and kissed her cheek. "We will be happy for you to join us. What happened is too many years ago to fret over."

Jane looked to Marilyn, who smiled and nodded. "It's only cold chicken with a Green Salad and Potato salad. Please stay."

"That's very kind of you."

Marilyn took charge of Jane showing her where the bathroom was. Then got on with preparing lunch. Jane found her way back out to sit down with me. "This is a lovely place." She remarked viewing the panorama of fields, valleys and small hills that could be seen from the patio.

"Yes. Marilyn's father bought it years ago. He knew what he was doing."

"Do you still work for..?" She couldn't remember the name of the company I had worked for.

"No. I work for myself now as a sort of technical advisor in court cases and complaints."

"Oh!"

I turned to look at her. "You should have phoned, Jane. It would have saved you a journey today, and we could have arranged another day for you to see Sarah."

"I know. We are only down here for a couple of days, and with Roger wanting to go off and see that railway, this really was the only chance I had. He refuses to have any contact with Sarah." She made it sound as if that was his choice rather than a Court Order. I bristled for a moment, but calmed quickly, it wasn't worth arguing about. She went on. "He's a good man really and a good provider." She was defending him.

"I'm sure he makes you happy."

"He does. It's just that he doesn't get on with Sarah. I know she gets on with Marilyn. I have never seen Sarah so happy when she came to get her things to come here."

"I suspect Jane, that had more to do with the horses, than Marilyn."

"Horses?"

"Yes. Sarah spends all of her free time at the stables down the lane."

Jane shook her head. "God! What kind of mother am I? I knew nothing about that."

Marilyn returned carrying a tray. "I thought we could eat out here. It's so nice; we should enjoy the weather while it lasts."

Jane got up saying. "Can I help?"

Marilyn nodded. "Yes. There are a couple more trays to bring out if you don't mind." I moved the table to the shade and arranged the chairs similarly. I couldn't help but think why Jane had come here. Yes, she could have wanted to see Sarah, but my antennae told me there was another reason as well. Was it simply feminine curiosity? That she wanted to see how I lived? If so she was probably disappointed, the cottage and gardens were sufficient to tell her that I was living a good life, and Jane would probably prefer that I lived in reduced circumstances. They returned and laid out lunch on the table. There was little said apart from general polite conversation over lunch.

Over coffee Jane felt compelled to speak. "Dal, I do want to see Sarah, but I also wanted to speak to you." She looked at Marilyn her attitude is asking for a private conversation, Marilyn then was about to get up.

I stopped her. "Jane if there is anything you want to say, say it now. Marilyn and I are a couple, I have never kept anything secret from her, and I will not start now." That got me a beaming smile from my wife and a grimace from my ex-wife.

"Ok. All I wanted to do was to apologize for mine and my family's treatment of you. You did nothing wrong, except get me pregnant, and it took two of us to do that. You stuck by me and all you got in return was disrespect, from me and my mother. I'm sorry. I am glad that you have found someone who loves you far more than I ever could, and that you are comfortable in your life." Now that was not what I was expecting. I was speechless for a while, taking that in, yet I still had the feeling that there was more to come. Jane had waited to see if I wanted to comment. She had probably allowed for that in her prepared speech and when I didn't say anything it disrupted her plans. "I would like to be able to see Sarah more, and possibly have her come and stay with me from time to time." I was happy for her to see Sarah, but not have Sarah stay with her.

"I have no objections to you seeing Sarah, but I think you will find that it's the Family Court you have to ask about her staying with you. They may wish to make conditions."

"Oh, you are not going on about that silly thing are you? We all know that those are lies. Roger wouldn't do anything like that."

Marilyn interrupted. "Did you actually talk to Sarah about that?"

"No. My mother did and she said Sarah was telling lies."

"And you took your mother's word for it?" Jane nodded.

I knew the signs; Marilyn was cocking both barrels and was going to fire soon. "Well, I did speak to Sarah. And she told me exactly what that pervert had tried to do and what he did do and I believe her. The police believed it too and that there was sufficient evidence there to go to Court. But you took your mother's word for it. A deceitful woman who knew all about your affair, and I suspect encouraged it, yet tried to suggest that it was Dal who was the unfaithful partner. A woman who was prepared to put her granddaughter into the care of a man who may well assault her sexually. And you! A mother who would turn a blind eye to the possibility that could happen. What a piece of work you are! Dal is being generous on agreeing that you could see Sarah, but as far as anything else is concerned, it is the Court which will make that decision."

"You are very opinionated for someone who has nothing to do with this."

I jumped in. "Wrong! The Court released Sarah into both our custody. I as her father and Marilyn as step-mother. She has as much to do with this as anyone else. Your inability to see the truth is alarming. You are much the same as your mother, who God knows would only see what she wanted to see and would adjust the facts for her convenience. Jane, thank you for your apology, but I am afraid that it means little if you are prepared to place our daughter in harm's way. You want to see Sarah? Go to Court and ask them to sanction it. I will not agree unless they order it so. And don't forget your daughter is now fourteen and the Court will listen to her."

The proceedings were interrupted by a cheery call from the lounge as Sarah arrived home. "Hello Mum." From where she was sitting Jane could not see Sarah and presumably Sarah could not know that her mother was here. She would only be able to see Marilyn. Jane's face was a picture as Sarah came out.

"Hi Dad." Then she saw who else was there. "Oh!"

"Hello Sarah." Said Jane. She went to get up, presumably to hug Sarah, but stopped when Sarah said.

"Hello Mother."

"It's Mum." Jane said.

Sarah shook her head. "You are my mother, but Marilyn is mum." Jane crumpled. Marilyn, who a few moments ago was prepared to tear her limb from limb went across and comforted her. Minutes later, Jane looked up at Sarah her face streaked with the tracks of her tears.

"I am your mum."

"Perhaps you haven't noticed that I have grown up. Who was it who explained all about periods to me, bought me pads and made sure that I knew how to cope with them. Marilyn! Who took me to get me my first bra? Marilyn! Who listened to me when I was frightened when your husband touched me? Not you mother, nor grandmother, who just told me I was a horrible deceitful girl who had made it all up. Neither of you who I could expect to listen to me, but Marilyn did, and she and dad did something about it. She is the closest person to a mum that I have." Jane's tears dripped down her cheeks. She pulled out a tissue and wiped them away. She got up and muttered "I'm sorry." and left. Marilyn followed her out to make sure she was alright.

I remonstrated with Sarah. "That wasn't very nice, Sarah. You knew your mother was here, didn't you?"

"Yes. I saw her car outside. I know dad. Shall I go after her and say sorry?"

I nodded. "I think that would be a good idea."

They seemed to be taking some time, so I got up and went through the lounge to look out of the front windows. Jane had opened her car door but hadn't got in. Marilyn was talking to her and Sarah was holding Jane's hand. Finally they seemed to have reached a conclusion and Marilyn with one last touch on Jane's arm left Sarah and her mother together. She came to join me. "Is she alright?" I asked.

"Yes. She has calmed down now. Sarah is talking with her. It's a bit traumatic when you have to face the fact that your mother is a lying, deceitful bitch, and that your husband is a sexual predator. She honestly believed that the whole thing about Sarah and Roger was made up. Now she knows the truth, and it isn't pleasant."

"No. I don't suppose it is. Should I go and talk with her?"

"I think that would be good. Let her know that you don't hold her personally responsible for how her mother acted."

Sarah and Jane were hugging each other when I approached them. Jane looked haunted and held out an arm to take my hand. Tears poured down her cheeks. "Dal, I am so sorry, so very sorry. I didn't know what was going on, and mum told me that Sarah was making it all up as she was jealous of Roger taking my time."

What do you say? It wasn't the time for crowing, telling someone that you were right all along. Particularly when the one person who you would believe had your daughter's interests at heart, turns out to be an evil bitch. "Come back inside. We'll have a cup of tea, or perhaps you would want something stronger, and you can wash your face."

Jane nodded and gave me a watery smile. "I'll pass on the something stronger, but I would like to repair my face."

Sarah grabbed her hand. "Come on mum. I'll show you where the bathroom is."

I went into the kitchen and put the kettle on. Marilyn joined me setting a tray for the cups and saucers.

"Sarah should see her mum from time to time." She told me.

"Yes." I agreed. "But if there is any chance that he will be there, then the answer is over my dead body."

"I don't think that Jane would consider that at all."

"Do you think she will leave him?" I speculated.

Marilyn shook her head. "No. She really loves him"

I thought about it and came to the conclusion that Marilyn was right. Jane had been with him for quite a few years now. I couldn't know how long she had been sleeping with him before we divorced, but I suspected that it was a long-term affair. It had culminated in their getting married, so it would appear that they were committed to each other. It was entirely possible that Jane would soon forget what he tried to do. I tried to explain my thoughts to Marilyn. She understood my reasoning, but didn't agree with it. The kettle was just starting to boil when she came up behind me and circled me with her arms.

Sarah returned alone, catching Marilyn hugging me. "Oh you two! Grow up will you?" We all laughed. "My mother has gone. She said she had embarrassed herself too much today already." She hesitated before asking a question. "Dad, I would like to see her from time to time, but I don't want to have any contact with him. Mother suggested that if she came down occasionally we could spend time together. Would you be upset about that?"

I wasn't too surprised. I had already envisaged something like that. "I have no problem with that." I turned to Marilyn. "What do you think?" Marilyn's eyes thanked me for including her.

"Sarah, she is your mother and you should see her, so phone her soon and tell her yes. We can make the arrangements when she can get down here." Then Marilyn's 'mum' role came to the fore. "You are still in your school uniform. Are you not going to change or are you starting to like the uniform?" Sarah pulled a face. She wore her uniform with an ill-grace preferring the ubiquitous fashion that all young girls affected now of Jeans and a T-shirt, so she went off to change.

Marilyn took the opportunity to pass on something she had gleaned from Jane. "From what Jane said, it would appear the she has known Roger far longer than you thought."

"Oh?" Marilyn nodded. "Well, do let on." I encouraged her.

"I gather that they were friends from their early teens. Your ex mother in law always thought that they would marry."

I poured tea whilst I thought about that. "That could explain a lot."

Marilyn seemed in agreement. "Are you thinking what I am thinking, or just thinking?" She asked.

"We are probably going down the same road. They were friends from their teens, possibly in love. Yet Jane for whatever reason gets herself pregnant and marries the father, me."

"Was Jane a virgin?" I nodded. Marilyn thought and then took my hypothesis further. "They meet again and become lovers, but she is married with a child. He has been denied that which he thought he would always get. Her virginity. And that is very important to some men. The understanding that no man has trespassed on what they see as their territory."

"Exactly." I hypothesized. "So when they do marry, he becomes fixated on the child who is almost a photocopy of the mother when she was young."

Marilyn was nodding her head and then said what I thought. "You can understand that. He is living with the woman he loves, yet the reincarnation of the young Jane is there every day to torment him. A virgin reincarnation to remind him of what he missed. The poor Bugger!" She hesitated a little. "He's still a bastard even so."

I was sipping my tea when Marilyn asked me a question that had me catch my breath. "Didn't it upset you that someone else took my virginity?"

I hadn't actually thought about that. I had to be honest with her. "I haven't thought about it, with twenty odd years between our first meeting and getting together again, it would be unusual for you to still be a virgin. After all, you are too much a catch not to attract attention. I had no thoughts of doing that when we first met. Just touching your breasts was as far as my ambitions went then. When we met again, it was understood that as we had both been married, then it followed that neither of us were virgins. That was in our pasts. In retrospect any upset would have been that we didn't find each other again."

She smiled. "That's my Dal. Turns an explanation into a positive. No wonder I love you so much." She came close and held me. "You have my little lady and my mouth. There is one virginity left." She whispered. "You can have that." I knew what she referred to and I have to say that the perversity did engage my loins pleasantly. She felt it and rubbed her belly sensuously against me. "I'll take that as a yes, shall I?"

"I would be less of a man to turn that down."

"Good. Perhaps we can schedule that for the future."

"The future! Why?"

Before she could answer, Sarah came into the kitchen now in her jeans and T-shirt. "Oh God! You two at it again?"

Marilyn laughed. "You'll learn, Sarah." She held out her arm to Sarah. "Come here, I have something to tell your dad so you may as well hear it at the same time." I was agog with curiosity. Sarah joined us. "I'm actually quite surprised, but it seems I am pregnant."

There was silence for a moment, and then Sarah cried. "Wheeeee! Fantastic." I was speechless, just standing there with a silly grin on my face.

Yes. Nineteen fifty seven was a very good year, so was nineteen seventy six, and it looks as if nineteen eighty is going to be good too.

~~The End~~

Here is a sample from another story you may enjoy:

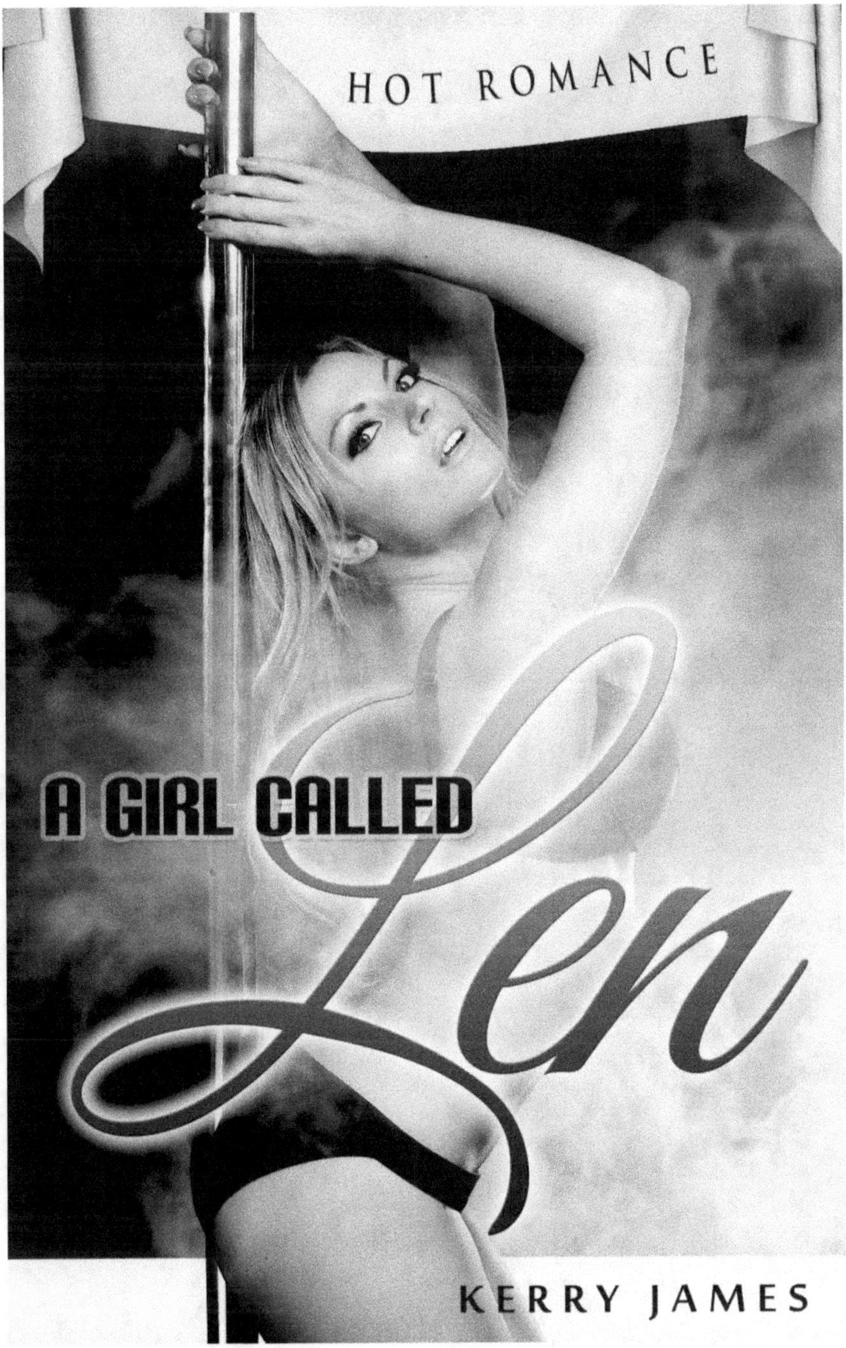
HOT ROMANCE
A GIRL CALLED
Len
KERRY JAMES

I fumbled my way through the dark club, apologising to the patrons as I stepped on toes, or bumped them and eventually found a seat quite close to the stage. I had paid a lot of money to be here, and I was going to get my money's worth. The stripper sort of danced to the recorded music, and gradually divested herself of her clothes. These she threw backwards to the wings of the stage. When she was down to just her skimpy panties, she stopped stripping and just sort of danced around the stage. At last, she started to slip them down, turning her back on the audience as they dropped below her hips. At that point, she wiggled and they fell to her ankles. Stepping out of them, she kicked them back to the wings, and then turned to face the audience, keeping one hand over the juncture of her thighs, listening to the music. At last, as the music came to its finale, she stood perfectly still with her legs tightly together and took her hand away, allowing us to see her pubic hair, but nothing else. She remained like that for about five seconds then the spotlights went out and the curtain drew.

I was to learn later that there were stringent rules as to what the girl could do and show on stage, and what she could not. I watched about three acts and whilst the way they got there varied, the last few seconds of the show were always the same. I knew that there were ten girls performing that night, and I was going to watch all of them. I was actually getting bored after seeing five or six of them, but I had paid to see the ten, I was bloody well going to see them. As patrons had left and seats became available I had managed to get nearer the stage, and just before the next act, a bloke got up from the very front and left. I was first into his still warm vacant seat.

Then the disembodied voice announced the next girl. "Ladies and gentlemen, we are proud to present the lovely Lee!" It seemed stupid to me to announce ladies and gentlemen, there was little chance of any women being in the audience. The curtains drew back and the spots came on to highlight the next stripper. Suddenly I went cold. My mind was playing tricks. It did look like her, but it couldn't be, I must be mistaken; after all, it was ten years since we last saw each other. She would have changed, and she would never be here taking her clothes off for a load of dirty old men. The irony that I was one among the forty or so of the dirty old men, passed me by completely. My front row seat meant that at certain times, as the moveable spot followed the girl around, my face would come into the splash of light. It was just what happened as the girl looked in my direction, and her face was shaken out of the bland uninterested look that all the girls seem to wear. Her routine took her away, but she looked over her shoulder as if to be certain. Then she turned in her dance, which had to be said was superior to the other dancers, and looked again.

At last, she seemed to come to a decision, so the next time she came to my side of the stage, she maneuvered much closer than before. She looked down at me, and from the side of her mouth a question came, "Danny?"

To buy the book, look for <u>**A Girl Called Len**</u>.

You may also like the books by these authors!

THE
PRODIGAL
Family
THE ABBOTTS

THE ABBOTTS: BOOK 1
EROTIC ROMANCE

Robert Courtney Abbott.   A forty-eight-year-old successful business man, married for twenty six years to Beverly Abigail Abbott, nee Sterns and with two children: Robert Courtney Abbott, Junior (affectionately called Deuce) and Stephanie Anne Abbott.

My wife Beverly is a vice president at a large advertising agency and it is that agency that I blame in large part for the current situation. Well, it is easier than taking the blame myself and besides, it is so much more comforting to put the blame elsewhere.

The Abbotts are a tad more than "slightly" well off, but I do so dislike the term "rich" so I settle for saying that we are "comfortable." Bev does not need to work, but she informed me early on that she intended to have a career and laid out my choices - a career-oriented Beverly or no Beverly at all. I do have to admit that if I knew back then that her career would put me in the situation that I now find myself in, I would still have chosen Beverly.

The Abbotts are health Nazis. We eat right, exercise religiously and as a result the four of us are in fine physical form, Beverly at forty-seven looks every bit of thirty-four and it pleases me that most people think that I'm not a day over thirty-six when in fact my half century mark is fast approaching.

Deuce is a recent college graduate with a degree in Electrical Engineering and he has chosen to go off and do his own thing rather than join the family business as I had hoped. I am disappointed, but it is his life so it gets to be his choice. Deuce lettered in every sport he put his hand to in high school, including some that I'd never even heard of, and still maintained an A average. He was offered athletic scholarships to a dozen well-known colleges and universities, but he turned them all down. He said he had enjoyed his childhood, but that it was now time to grow up and prepare for his future as a man and he buckled down and went to work on a degree in Electrical Engineering at the college close to home.

Stephanie Anne is in her final year at Smith and I believe that she is majoring in Economics, but I can't really be sure since she has changed majors so often. Deuce says that the only major that Steph really pursues is popularity. I think the boy is a tad jealous. Steph has been surrounded by swains since she was thirteen. She is drop dead gorgeous just like her mother, a straight A student and she lettered in track in high school and plays soccer and field hockey now that she is in college.

All of the above to offer just the briefest of glimpses of the Abbotts and now to the current situation that I find myself in.

***

We need to go back eighteen months to set the stage. We own a summer house on the lake and every August we go there for a three-week vacation. That particular August there were four of us at the summer house. Stephanie Anne was off backpacking in Europe with some friends. Deuce had brought along his fiancée Amber and then there was Bev and me.

Amber was a gorgeous young creature and an absolute joy to the eyes when she wore her bikinis - especially her "wicked weasels" - and my ribs were still sore a month later from all the elbows that Bev kept jabbing in my ribs whenever she caught me looking at Amber. Of course, Bev looked just as fantastic in her bikini so between Bev and Amber I was in an almost constant state of erection and I was more than happy to share those erections with my lovely wife.

Two weeks went by and then one Tuesday Bev received a phone call from her agency. There was a major problem with one of their largest and most important accounts and they needed her to return to work as soon as possible. Forty-five minutes later she was gone and there I was with no one to share my Amber-generated erections with.

Wednesday, Deuce and Amber hooked up with some kids on the other side of the lake and went to a party. I spent part of the day out on the lake fishing and the rest of it lounging around. I went to bed around ten with a book and half an hour later I was asleep.

According to the bedside clock it was two-thirty in the morning when the hot mouth on my cock woke me up. That was one of Bev's favorite tricks when she was horny and I was asleep. She would wake me with a blow job and once I was stiff enough to suit her she would attempt to turn me into a ruined wreck. Obviously she had just gotten back from the city and was horny. Once I was awake I grabbed her and maneuvered her over me in a sixty-nine and went to work on her pussy. She moaned as my tongue delved into her and she pushed her pussy down at me. I munched on her muffin and she moaned around my cock in her mouth. I worked on her pussy for several minutes and was surprised when she had an orgasm. Bev rarely has an orgasm when I eat her so I guessed she must have been super horny.

She was still shaking from her climax when I moved behind her and eased my cock into her. Bev shoved back at me which told me that she wanted me to go fast and hard so I gripped her hips with both hands and drove into her. Because of the time she had spent on my cock I was only able to go five or six minutes, but it was long enough for me to bring her off once more. I pulled out and fell to the bed next to her and put my arms around her, expecting some snuggle time, but she pulled away from me, swung around and went for my cock again. She moved over me in a sixty-nine and it dawned on me what was happening.

It wasn't the first time that it had happened and when it did it made her extremely horny. Bev was a hot-looking babe and she got hit on a lot. Every once in a while a really hot guy would make a determined run at her and while she deflected the pass, it nonetheless made her horny as hell. While she was in the city, someone must have made a move on her.

I dug into her pussy and worked on it and damn if I didn't give her another orgasm. By then I was stiff again so I fucked her for about ten minutes giving her two more orgasms before I had mine. This time when I pulled her to me she moved in tight and we fell asleep.

Daylight was coming in through the window and I was in that half awake- half asleep state when I heard "Oh shit!" I opened my eyes and saw not Bev, but Amber. She was looking at me wide-eyed…

To buy the book, look for **The Prodigal Family: The Abbotts**.

Jack Ryder

LOVING
My Sitter
Down and Dirty MILF
Hot Erotica

Aunt Marci wasn't really my aunt. At least, not biologically. She and my mother grew up in a foster home together and became very close. By the time they grew up and moved out on their own, they thought of each other as sisters. This continued even after mom got married and moved away with her new soldier husband. She always considered Marci her little sister.

Mom ended up being a single mother when my father was killed during a routine training mission. It was one of those fluke accidents that can happen when you've got a bunch of young men running around in a wooded area with guns and live ammunition. It was supposed to be a routine recon mission. But the men got spooked by reports that there were bears in the area. Dad was shot just at dusk by a young kid that mistook him for a bear.

I can't really say that being an only child of a single mother was difficult in any way. I never knew my dad and aunt Marci sort of filled that void during my early years. Despite being in her early teens, she was a wonderful nanny during those years. It provided mom the time to go back to school to complete her college courses. I always felt close to Marci even as a young boy.

By the time I reached my first year of college, mom had gotten her nursing degree and then her PHD in medical education. Marci had also earned her master's degree in nursing just before we moved away. I did not get to see Marci very often over the next two years. Mom accepted a professorship at a University in Oklahoma and Marci became a nurse at home in Ogden, Utah.

I won't bore you with everything that happened while I lived in Oklahoma, but there are a few significant things that I must pass on here. The first thing that happened was that I discovered that I could throw a baseball pretty well. I guess to be accurate I should tell you that I was soon considered a "Phenom" by the end of my first year of college. By the time the second year began, I already had pro offers and pro baseball scouts following me around.

As a result of my new found fame and notoriety, I also had a parade of young gorgeous girls that made it very obvious that they would drop their panties for me. This led to my second discovery. I loved the attention of women! But the weird thing was that I found most of the girls my age too shallow. I also found them too self-involved to ever measure up to the support and genuine nurturing that I had received from Marci and my Mother.

It was also during these two years that it finally occurred to me how absolutely sexy my nanny Marci was. I had not really ever thought about her in that way until she came to visit us that first Christmas after we moved away. Mom was working late those last couple of days before the Christmas break and I spent most of those evenings alone with Marci.

From the moment she came in the front door that first day of her two-week vacation, I could hardly take my eyes off of her. It was like my eyes were seeing her for the first time and what I saw was a tremendously sexy young woman. At five foot one, her 32D-22-33 figure made her an absolute little bombshell.

Her shoulder length auburn hair was long enough that if she let it fall forward, it could just cover her breasts. Like any true redhead, her skin is a soft milky white with little patterns of freckles on various locations. Her amber brown eyes look gold in the direct sunlight. Her full pouty lips make you wish you could kiss her endlessly.

I had an erection within minutes after she arrived that first evening. I did my best to conceal it as I carried her luggage into the house for her. I turned red as a beet when I saw her gaze between my legs as I dropped her luggage on the floor in the guest bedroom. I was relieved that she did not say anything about it as we went to the kitchen to make dinner.

I had an erection the entire time that I watched her cook our spaghetti dinner. Her perfectly round ass looked so damn sexy in the tight faded jeans that she had on. I found myself wishing I was twelve years older as I fantasized about pulling those jeans down and bending her over that counter top. I could almost swear that she found ways to wiggle her ass while she was going about her cooking. My dick would twitch each time she did it.

It appeared to me that a couple more buttons on her blouse were unfastened when she sat down at the table to eat. I could now see just the top of her frilly black bra. Because it was also a see through type material, I could clearly see the tops of her gorgeous milky breasts. It took every bit of my self-control to not stare at her tits while we ate.

I made small talk as we ate in an attempt to keep my mind off what it really wanted to focus on. I can honestly say that Marci was the very first girl I ever fantasized about. It started that evening as we ate dinner. My eyes secretly memorized every curve of her body, the small bumps in the center of her breasts, the way her pouty lips seemed to pulse as she ate her food.

"I heard that you are the star pitcher of your college baseball team." Marci's voice broke through a momentary vision of me fondling her tits. I felt a small ooze of fluid into my shorts as I lifted my eyes from her tits to her face. She was grinning slightly. "Yes...I do...Okay," I stammered as I felt a warmth radiating in my face.

"I guess that means you're good with your hands," she giggled playfully as she raised her fork to her mouth. I felt my dick twitch as she slowly placed the fork in her mouth then very sensually pulled it back out with her pouty lips pressed down on the tangs. "Yes...I guess....I am." I felt a shiver go up my spine as she slowly licked her lips then used her napkin to dab at the corners of her luscious mouth.

If you enjoyed this sample then look for **Loving My Sitter**.

GEORGE X. BUSH

AFFAIRS
Conundrum
ATONEMENT

WIFE SHARING EROTICA

John Rutter approached his front door very weary from his day's work. A last-minute meeting had pushed his day into overtime and at 8pm he was just getting home. As he entered, he was surprised to hear voices from within as he set his briefcase down. Walking into the living room, he was even more surprised to see his boss, Horace Ender, and his wife, Emma, along with the ubiquitous presence of Horace's bodyguard/right-hand man, Jared, all 6'8" and 275 pounds of sculpted black imperviousness. Even more jarring was the presence of Horace's secretary, Melissa, a 5'4" red-headed pixie with an upturned, freckled nose beneath bright green eyes.

"So, you're finally home," Jean, John's wife said, pressing her body into his and kissing him lightly on the lips. "Busy day?" she asked, her bright green eyes staring into his as her braless breasts rubbed lightly against his chest, her waist-length blonde hair swaying back and forth.

"Very," John replied, still wondering how he could have forgotten that everyone was coming over this evening.

"Sorry to surprise you, John," Horace said, at 65 still a silver-haired, energetic powerhouse of a man whose 6'3" frame was dwarfed by the presence of Jared standing behind him.

"Not at all," John replied, nonplussed. "I thought I had forgotten you were coming or something."

"Hello, John," Emma said, her silvery-grey hair tied back in a ponytail just like her husband's. At 63 and 5'6", Emma Ender was still a beautiful, willowy woman with bright blue eyes. "Nice to see you again."

"Emma," John replied, taking her hand and kissing her on both cheeks. "My pleasure. You look great," he said, admiring her and her husband, both very tanned from spending so much time at their home in Hawaii. "To what do we owe the pleasure?" he asked.

"Your future, John," Horace replied, a firm look on his face.

"My future?" John said a bit nervously.

"Yes," Horace answered. "Why don't you sit down and we'll talk," he said, indicating the large seat next to him.

As John settled nervously into the seat, everyone else settled down, too, Jean sitting between Melissa and Emma on the sofa while Jared stood behind John imposingly.

"Now see here, John," Horace began. "As far as your work goes, I can't say we've ever had a better, more productive employee, so rest assured on that score."

"I'm happy to hear it," John replied.

"Your energy, innovative thinking, and enthusiasm have all combined to bring in much business," Horace said. "So naturally we think of promoting you. We like to keep the best and the brightest and most promising at all costs."

"Wow, I don't know what to say," John said, truly surprised that this moment had come after only 2 years with the company.

"But we also consider other factors," Horace continued, "in deciding which people are worth keeping, factors such as honesty, morality, and suitability to our particular type of corporate culture. Being a productive worker just isn't enough anymore in today's marketplace."

"I understand," John replied.

"We're interested in determining whether you're such a person," Horace said. "But we do have some reservations, I must admit, which is why we're here tonight."

"What do you mean?" John asked, struggling to keep the nervousness from his voice.

"Well, we like to know that managers in our company are honest, truthful, and can be relied upon at all times, as well as whether they fit into our particular corporate culture," Horace said. "Are you such a person, John? Are you honest and truthful? Do you fully fit into our particular type of corporate culture? Can you be relied upon at all times to do what is required of you and do so with the utmost in discretion? Now, think before you answer. This is extremely important. Everything about your future with the company depends upon how you respond this evening."

Everyone just watched John expectantly, saying nothing. The tension was so thick you could cut it with a knife.

"The best answer I can give you," John replied after due consideration, "is that I always try to be honest and truthful. I'm not a saint and I don't always succeed, but it's important to me, too, so I try. As for being reliable and acting with discretion as far as the company is concerned, 150%," he stated. "I have to say that I've never had a job that was as challenging, yet as exciting and fun. I look forward to going to work each and every day."

"Yes, that we're well aware of," Horace said somewhat cryptically. "But we're referring to your entire life when we talk about honesty and truthfulness and integrity, and even to an extent our particular corporate culture. Was your answer only about work or did it also cover your life in general?"

"My life, period," John answered without hesitation.

"I see," Horace said, a disturbed look on his face.

"John, when we got married, we agreed to always be open and honest with each other, to share our lives completely," Jean said from her seat on the sofa. "No matter what."

"That's right," John agreed, nodding his head warily.

"Neither of us were virgins when we met, but I've been absolutely faithful to you ever since we got married," she continued.

"Can you say the same, John?" Emma asked quietly from the sofa.

John just stared at the three of them sitting there, realizing suddenly that both Melissa and Emma were each holding one of Jean's hands.

"No," John replied quietly after a minute. "I can't say the same."

"I'm glad you're being honest with us, John," Horace said after a few moments of pregnant silence filled the room. "That's very important, believe me. Now, you're saying you've been unfaithful to your wife; is that correct?"

"Yes," John replied, hardly daring to look Jean in the face but not daring to look anywhere else.

"Has it been one woman, many women?" Horace asked.

"Just one," John answered.

"I see," Horace said, nodding his head. "And was this a one-time thing or an ongoing thing?"

"It's been ongoing," John admitted, hating the look of pain in Jean's eyes as she stared at him, white-knuckled as she held Melissa & Emma's hands.

"Are you in love with this other woman?" Horace asked.

"No," John answered, exhaling a huge breath. "It's just sex, lust."

"Your wife doesn't please you, satisfy you sexually enough?" Emma asked softly.

"Oh, no, it has nothing at all to do with Jean," John exclaimed. "I'm totally, 100% committed to her. I love her. Our sex life is good, great. I never leave the house without..." he said, then stopped as he realized he was saying too much.

"Without what?" Emma asked, a smile almost creasing her face.

"Without, without..." John tried to say.

"Without fucking me," Jean filled in. "And when he gets home, that's usually the first thing that happens, we fuck. That's why I don't understand..."

"And if saving your marriage and your job, depended upon you stopping this behavior immediately, would you? Could you?" Horace asked.

"Yes," John replied emphatically. "My marriage and job are far more important to me."

"And you'd be willing to atone for your transgressions if need be?" Horace asked.

"Yes, if that's what's necessary," John said, nodding his head, feeling the sweat on his brow even though it was a cool evening and the windows were open.

"How shall you atone?" Horace asked almost rhetorically. "Is it possible to atone for this?" he asked, reaching down and picking up the remote control and pointing it at the television and pushing a button.

John stared in astonishment as a side-by-side picture of his office appeared on the television, one view being from the door, the other from the wall behind his desk facing the door. No part of his office was hidden from view.

"Shall we get started," John's voice came from the television, followed almost immediately by John himself with Melissa trailing…

To buy the book, look for **Affairs, Conundrum, Atonement**.

G. Stuart Crane

The Flog Zone

Paranormal Precognition

BDSM Erotic Romance

John Peters didn't know what his first birth was like, but his second one was agonizing. He remembered the pain, the drowsy driver crossing lanes, the sounds of crushing and crumpling metal and glass, the fire, and the screaming of his lungs out as they were seared by the very air he breathed. This passed and he felt a new sensation of someone using his/her hands to move his legs. Then came the hot kiss of a lash, and he felt as if he were being flogged forever when he tried to open his eyes to scream. Then the pain turned to pleasure and as it continued till the lash fell.

The scream came out as a gurgle, a whisper. His eyes opened to see light blue walls all around him and that he was in a bed. A woman in surgical scrubs was moving his legs and feet, stretching them, moving them back and forth at the ankles and knees. The woman was pleasant, not pretty in the formless clothes she wore, but with her red hair back in a short ponytail. Expressive green eyes is now wide and watching him. She had stopped what she was doing and was watching a machine beside him. The steady *beep beep* was replaced by something wilder and erratic.

As soon as the woman lets go of his foot, the sensation of being flogged stopped. The combined sensation of pain and pleasure stopped and the machine keeps beeping at a faster pace. She had rushed to his side, and was watching him struggle to form words with his mouth that no longer seemed to work. The noises coming from his mouth were just gargles and hisses.

She left in a hurry and somehow the presence of the fast beeping machine beside him was not an acceptable trade. Still trying to form words, he croaked for help. Where the heck was he and what was happening?

He managed to move his head a little, and look towards left and right. He was in a hospital ward of some kind and bodies on beds were to the left and right of him. Still with IV bags on stands and tubes everywhere, he was sure that he was unmoved. He tried to move his arms and found his arms free and couldn't move a little, since he was so weak.

Minutes passed, the silence was incredible except for the steady drone of the machines and the low beeping noises from all around him. The silence was replaced by the sound of footfalls. He heard hard soled shoes and squeaky rubber ones on tiled floors, walking in a hurry. A nurse in a white uniform and a man in a lab coat flapping behind were at his side. He was older, judging by the wrinkles and gray hair.

"You are awake?" the man in a lab coat asked.

He tried to say "Yes I am and where am I?" but all that came out was a series of croaks and guttural sounds. He did see a name embroidered on the lab coat stating that his name was D. Burns M.D.

He looked at John a few moments, then told the nurse to get some water and straw. He waited till she returned. He poured some room temperature water in a glass, added the straw, and held it to John's lips.

John sucked in the fluid and his mouth seemed to absorb it before the liquid got to his cheeks. The second pull on the straw was better and it got into his throat with the same effect. The third pull went down his throat and soon the dryness and tickling was gone. He pushed the straw away with his tongue and tried to speak again. This time, it came out in a whisper, but intelligible for his ears, it sounded weak and pitiful. "Where am I and how long have I been here?"

The Doctor had to lean closer to hear him. "We will get to that soon, but do you remember your name?"

John whispered his full name to the doctor, then sighed, this was going to be a memory test. Then, while he could, he rattled off his address and anything else that came to mind including his high school and college. The doctor pulled back to look at him. "And what's the last thing you remember?"

"Car, a big white SUV crossing the center line, I couldn't avoid it. I tried running my car onto the sidewalk, it happened fast, the fire, and me screaming." John managed to whisper. "What about my car?"

If you enjoyed this sample then look for **The Flog Zone.**

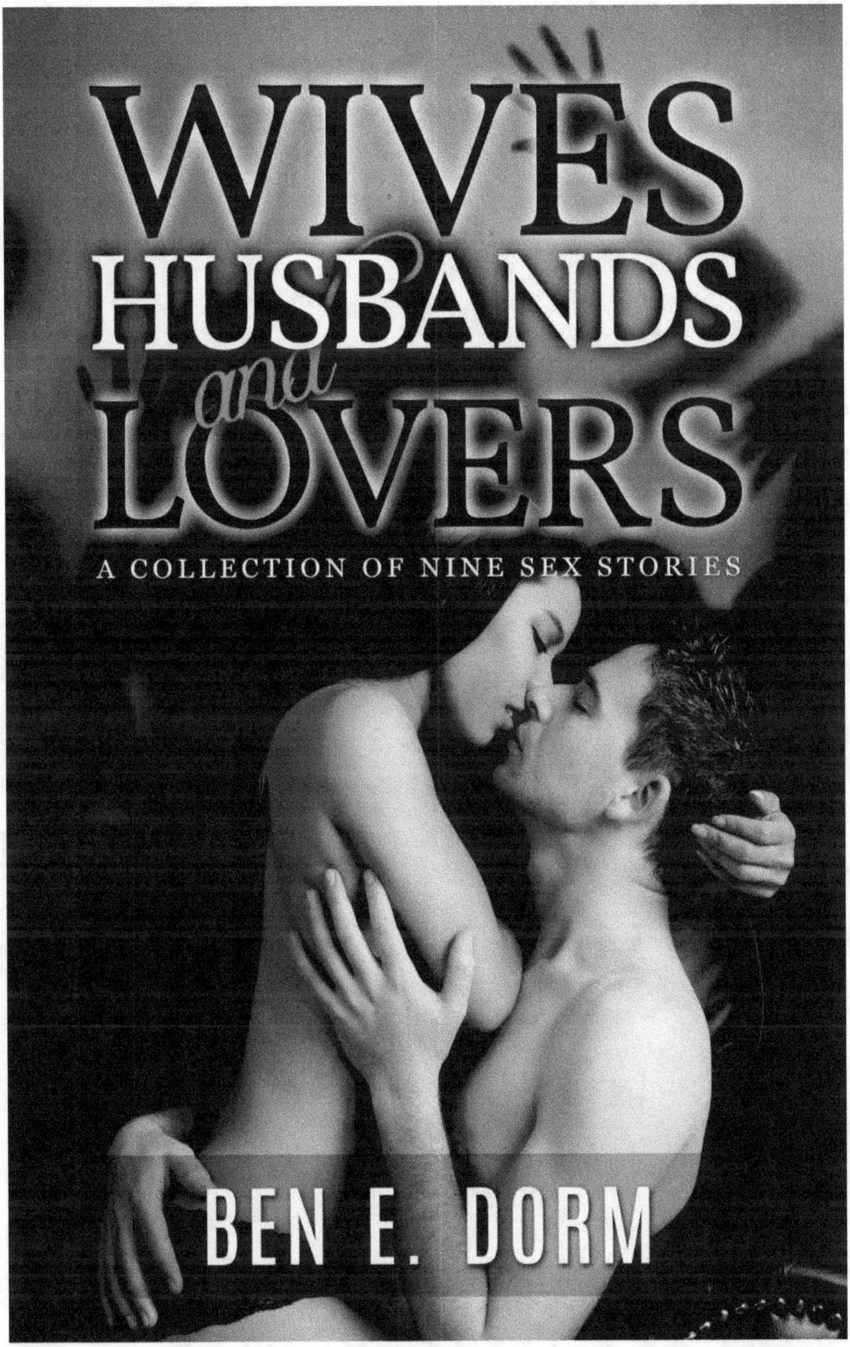
WIVES
HUSBANDS
and
LOVERS
A COLLECTION OF NINE SEX STORIES
BEN E. DORM

The audacity of the question caught Barbara by surprise. She blinks and gulps at her drink, then eventually splutters because she forgot it was wine in the glass. Swigging the stuff down like water was a mistake.

Struggling, Barbara stammers, "I... uh... I mean to say, Tuh-Tanya..." The heat rises in her face and she falls silent. Barbara doesn't have the words to respond. Her mouth hangs open while thoughts collide in a discordant jumble of conflicting impressions.

Everything is all furred up by the afternoon wine. *Dear God*, she thought, *it must be a bottle each by now!*

Barbara eyes, an offending article, a bottle of Sauvignon Blanc sat on the low table in front of her. Rather blurry, Barbara shifts on the very large, very comfortable three-seater sofa. She realizes that it's the third bottle, but it registers vaguely.

Slack-faced she lifts her face towards her host when Tanya cajoles her with, "Come on, Babs. Don't be shy. It's just a laugh."

Looking at the younger woman – who seems unaffected by so much drink – Barbara sees mischievous eyes twinkling in Tanya's elfin face. She takes in the detail of Tanya's platinum-blonde bobbed hair, dark roots visible in a central parting which, she believes, are the season's *de-rigueur*. She thinks dark roots are a particularly trampy look, but acknowledges Tanya carries it off well. In Barbara's estimation her host is a very pretty girl, but the understanding is slowly dawning and Barbara is coming to realize the innocence the young woman projects are rather misleading.

Barbara thinks the tramp style might be appropriate as she lowers her appraisal to Tanya's generous bosom beneath the tight, button-fronted blouse and smart, waist-length fawn jacket. A high-hemmed skirt rides up to Tanya's thighs, exposing a lot of bare, gym-toned and pleasantly tanned leg and Barbara is suddenly even more self-conscious when confronted with Tanya's physical appeal.

"Oh, Tanya, I don't know if that's entirely appropriate..." says Barbara, her tone stiff and pompous. She gulps more wine and wonders how the Liverpudlian girl can be so confident and self-assured, envy at Tanya's effervescence mixing in with what she perceives as her own repressed and strait-laced character.

Tanya's eyes roll as she says, "You won't shock me, Babs. I could tell you things I've done..." Then Tanya's glance flicks to Barbara's empty glass. "A top up?" she asks, reaching for the bottle.

"Oh, God, Tanya, I shouldn't. It's only three o'clock..."

But Barbara soon finds herself holding yet another brimming glass while Tanya grins at her.

"So, come on, Barbara," the blonde insists. "Tell me – what's the dirtiest thing you've ever done? Ever been to an orgy?"

Enough is enough, Barbara decides. "Of course not!" she gasps, bristling with indignation. "How absurd!"

Unfazed, Tanya laughs and continues with, "A threeway, then? Ever had two blokes at the same time?" Her expression turns vulpine, pale-blue eyes narrowing to match the sly grin Tanya fixes on Barbara. "A man and another woman?" Tanya adds, sipping wine, attention rapt and fixed on Barbara's face.

Barbara gasps again. "Tanya, please!" Her mouth opens and closes as she struggles with the disconcerting effects of afternoon drinking and the shocking interview. The wine combined with a totally unexpected line of questioning has her struggling for composure. This *isn't* what she's used to at all. "Why do you insist on embarrassing me?" she breathes.

Tanya laughs again before smiling at Barbara, her look contrite.

Holding up a conciliatory hand, Tanya says, "Okay, Babs, I'm sorry. I didn't mean any offense. I'm just a gobby cow. Always have been. I'm only teasin' ya."

It's the girl's accent, her blonde hair, the confidence and her youth that goads Barbara into revealing more than she knows is wise. Despite Tanya being at least fifteen years her junior, Barbara, at just over forty, feels so staid and unworldly – so bloody middle-class and *suburban*. She knows it's unwise but, fuddled with drink and confronted with Tanya's supposed contrition, Barbara feels obliged to blurt her innermost and very intimate fantasies.

"Well," she says, voice low as she avoids Tanya's eyes, "if you must know…"

To buy the book, look for **Wives, Husbands and Lovers**.

WANT FREE COPIES OF MY BOOKS?
Just visit my blog and download free copies of my books:
http://kerry-james.awesomeauthors.org/

www.ingramcontent.com/pod-product-compliance
Lightning Source LLC
Chambersburg PA
CBHW071410170626
46811CB00003B/1335